Entering Through the Narrow Gate

A Novel

PATTIE TREBUS

authorHOUSE®

AuthorHouse™
1663 Liberty Drive
Bloomington, IN 47403
www.authorhouse.com
Phone: 1 (800) 839-8640

Published by AuthorHouse 07/16/2015

ISBN: 978-1-4969-7452-5 (sc)
ISBN: 978-1-4969-7451-8 (e)

Library of Congress Control Number: 2015903520

Print information available on the last page.

CHAPTER ONE

November 2012

The rumbling from the 6:30 am train usually woke me each morning at this same time; and from sleep that left me more tired in the morning than when I went to bed. Plagued by insomnia, I didn't think that I had ever really slept soundly. I could recall as a young child getting up in the middle of the night to draw pictures on the wall and getting punished for it the next day. My parents would eventually paint over the wall and I never understood the real damage. But in my abode now the distant sounds were so far away -- as my attention toward it increased, it seemed to be pushing and humming along outside my bedroom window. Cha-choo, cha-choo. Its pounding and barreling along reminded me of the sounds that I used to hear while growing up on a farm in Virginia. I wonder where those happy and carefree times went. Hearing the train many miles away represented the stillness and tranquility in the country. Now, suburbia here in Ohio is bustling with teenagers' loud cars and annoying music blaring from stereos. Yet, there is still in the early morning hours, birds outside my window chirping incessantly and pecking until I am too awake to go back to sleep. Neighbors constantly complain about the birds residing in the shutters, but as I've heard, birds living in or near your home is a sign of good luck, and if that's the case, then I should have a lot of it.

Today was my 39th birthday—not a big birthday, but a little closer to 40... and I didn't care. As I awoke, bleary-eyed and not ready to begin the day, I pondered what I could do today. I had no big plans. That was the problem –nothing to do since I no longer had my full-time teaching position. Just an adjunct teaching position, but something nevertheless that brought in a little spare change. I had this weird feeling that I couldn't shake that something out of the ordinary would happen, but I couldn't fathom what. I brought my thoughts back to what I needed to do today to get my life back into some semblance of normalcy. I was planning to stay home and watch a good movie and talk to friends who would be calling me to wish me a happy birthday. And I had my miniature collie, Sylva, whose name meant "rest," that spent hours lounging in the living room, curled up on the loveseat. I would swear that dog could understand everything that she saw on TV. If Law and Order came on, she would crouch down and put her head down, seemingly mesmerized by the action and intently pricking her ears up whenever she heard the ba-boom,for each scene. Sylva means "rest" so the name was appropriate for a lap dog whose only skill was in discerning a person's intentions. She would convey her approval or disapproval with a lick, a slight turn of the head, and a nudge if she approved, and a grimacing of teeth if she disapproved. She also loved licking my fingers after I had just made some fried chicken. So anything she did was adorable to me and I loved her nonetheless. I was content to stay home and be alone, although secretly I wished that I had someone who would surprise me with a romantic evening with my soul mate whoever he was. But that wasn't meant to be – at least not this year.

My mind was reveling in this silly fantasy when the pounding on my door and doorbell made my arms jump and my head snap from my pillow. Funny I thought,

"Oh, here's the big surprise that I was just imagining and daydreaming about. Who on earth was paying me a visit?" Funny it was the man that I had been dreaming about the night before. Slightly dizzy, I pushed the blinds open just enough to see an unmarked car and two men who looked like they were here for official investigation.

Looking around my bedroom, I threw on some old sweatpants and sweatshirt and rushed down the hall, panting and knowing that this was serious. In my socks, I slipped down the carpeted steps, unlocked the door to find the two men holding FBI badges –both with ominous expressions. I pretended to check out their badges but was too nervous to actually look at the details of the black and gold-lined badges set in plastic covers that they scooped in their palms as if not to allow in the neighborhood to see . . . . but still conspicuous. I unlocked the door and allowed them to come in. They simultaneously put their badges away, and pulled open the storm door that swung open on it squeaky and oily hinges. After a quick look, the men immediately put their hands in their pockets and peered at me with such inquisitiveness as if to bore a hole in my eyes. I looked the two men over wondering why they would unexpectedly show up on my doorstep . . . Two FBI agents in my home. Unable able to breathe. One breath, two breaths, three breaths.

"Madison Hauck," Yes, I nodded.

The brusque man on the left said, "Ms. Hauck, we'd like to ask you some questions."

They followed me up the stairs in two seconds flat. The stout man on the left lagged behind at the door while the lean man on the right swished in and trudged up the steps behind me at an uncomfortably close distance. The bottom of his coat swished as the tips touched the back of my calves. I could feel his eyes staring at my body, and turning my head slightly over my shoulder, I could see that he was indeed checking me out from top to bottom. An agent, but still a man. And men will sneak a peek if they can.

He said matter-of-factly, "We have to check out everything that is reported to us, no matter what it is –that's our duty. And we talk to *a lot* of people."

I said, "I bet." I somehow implied that the *other* people they interviewed were different than I was. They made their way up to the steps for a series of questions that would only be the beginning of the tumult to come.

CHAPTER TWO

Trailing me at the top of the steps and around the bannister, the first agent took a sigh and said, "Nice home." He looked at every wall and at the furniture and decorations with Polish pottery dishes, hanging plates, and tea pitchers on a round, glass table covered with ivory linens. The other agent was bending over and looking over my shoes on the pine shoe stand near the front door. It seemed so curious to me to be inspecting my shoes with such deliberateness, but then again, he was trained to be a detective. Stacked in neat rows with winter shoes on the top shelf, fall shoes in the middle, and summer shoes on the bottom, were four tiers of all my footwear – from boots to tennis shoes to sandals – only my shoes were on the rack since I lived alone. What he could find out by checking out my shoes, I didn't know.

The first agent took a seat on the sofa while the second agent made his way up the steps and sat down next to him. I pulled a chair from the living room in front of them and sat down. The first agent introduced himself, "My name is Agent Nelson, and I need to ask you about the time you spent teaching at University of Cincinnati." Tall and handsome, he was 50-ish with his grooved face displayed crow's feet around the eyes, a seasoned detective. He showed a serious demeanor, a man who could take control of a situation. His slicked-backed, dirty blonde hair and chiseled face was the epitome of someone with years of investigatory experience. He wore stone-black pants covered with a gray trench coat.

His partner said, "I'm Agent Garrett, and I received information that there were threats floating around on campus. They appear to be from the international students, and we needed to clear up what may or may not be a possible threat to national security. Is that correct?"

I said, "Who told you about the threats at UC?"

Agent Nelson said, "Actually, it was from a tip that we received from the EEOC. This person stated that we should identify who is behind some of the hate crimes or whatever is taking place on campus. We just need to get some brief information first."

"Whatever you need to know, I'll try to answer as best I can."

Agent Garrett's attire was more casual with navy blue pants and a worn, dark brown leather jacket. His boyish, suntanned face was muscular and chiseled. Tall and strong, he towered over me and the other agent, and he looked like a former football player. His wavy, slick dark hair was attractive and masculine. From his physique, he probably played football in high school or college. There was some quality about his speaking that emanated shyness and timidity which was very appealing. His voice seemed more gentle and kind than the other agent and he rustled through the papers to read over the specifics of the report that I sent them. Shuffling through his papers and organizing papers, Agent Nelson took the lead in questioning me. With his right brow turned upward and his head turned slightly, he was now in full question mode.

"How long have you lived here in Cincinnati?"

"Um, about a year and a half."

"What did you teach at UC and how long did you teach there?"

"I taught English Composition at UC."

"Tell us what exactly happened that prompted us to receive this complaint from the EEOC. We *need* to know."

Nervous at recounting my story, my lips started shaking and I became aware of my trembling hands which I clenched to mask my obvious anxiety. I was overcome with nervousness – two agents who were giving me their full attention. And I knew that they could read my every twitch for truthfulness. Agent Nelson leaned forward while gripping his hands. He was intent on hearing every word that I had to say. For some odd reason, it wasn't what you would expect from an FBI agent. Agent Garrett clicked his pen and turned over the pages on his clipboard. He was eager to take notes, and I was eager to tell my story.

"I was terrorized by a Saudi Arabian student. I was also bullied and threatened by a UC supervisor and by the administration, so I had to resign to get out of that horrendous job. I was a whistleblower about the grade changing and my snitching on colleagues who were feeding the students questions so they could memorize the answers before the exams."

Agent Nelson said, "But if some student was threatening you, why would the Administration *not* want that guy outta there ASAP?" Silence. Tension in the air.

"All for the money," I admitted. "If they can't keep the money comin' in, then they lose their jobs."

Agent Garrett piped in, "So the guy was out to get some revenge on you?"

"Yeah, I muttered." Both agents let out a sigh and looked down, in disgust.

"Describe him to us. How old was he and what did he look like?"

"He was young, early 20s, and he had curly hair that was stringy and hung out of this old blue cap."

"Tell us about his features."

"He had dark olive skin and a rather small build." Questions starting flying like darts hitting a board.

"Now, why did he threaten you?"

Pressing my lips together, I said, "He threatened me because I wouldn't play the University game – that is, allowing him to pass so they can get the tuition."

"And what game is that? What exactly did he say?'

My voice strengthened. "A student can fail the final exam and still argue that he should pass. I suppose that's the norm in Middle Eastern countries. Saudi students told me that they have every right to cheat if they can get away with it." My eyes watered making it look like I was about to cry – but they were tears of frustration.

Agent Garrett asked, "Did any of the other students get the same deal. Were you coerced into cheating for others too?"

"Never," I said. With that, Agent Garrett clicked his pen off, set it inside the folder, and closed it.

Agent Nelson sighed and said, "Is that it?"

Frustrated, I added, "He got in my face, yelled at me, and pushed my shoulder against the wall."

"Why wouldn't they act ASAP?" Agent Garrett asked.

They shook their heads back and forth in disgust. They *knew* all right -- knew that I had been threatened, that the university was trying to coerce me into changing grades. All I knew was that I was scared of facing an aggressive student bent on getting the grade that he wanted, not what he earned.

"He would lose his student visa on account of his failing grade – and blame it all on me."

Agent Nelson might have been the inquisitive detective at the beginning, but now he was scrunching down as if he didn't know what to do – and this made him more human, softer, and more protective.

Finally, there was someone who would listen to the truth in what I was telling them.

I felt better and I was able to get myself together. The facts, which had been buried, were now being uncovered and unearthed like coal being brought up from the dank and dingy underground.

Agent Garrett asked, "So who was your supervisor and why didn't she step in to stop this harassment?"

"My supervisor was Loretta Bryson, and she didn't do anything about it because she was in on the scheme to keep as many international students at UC – the Saudi students – who paid bags of money for grades."

"Why would any university keep any student threatening others?" Garrett continued.

Conciliatory, I said, "It's about our relationship with another country – political ties and money. It's not only about money but in keeping a diplomatic front."

Agent Garrett asked, "Why couldn't you go to some higher ups?"

Frustrated at having to justify my inaction, I said, "She ordered me to change grades and not rat on her to anyone about the massive cheating scandal. She insinuated that I'd be sorry if I told *anyone.* It was all a big scheme." I realized that after I said the word "scheme" that the two agents would conclude that I was overreacting to the intimidation.

Agent Nelson said annoyingly, "Don't you think that Ms. Bryson's motive was just to cover up a bad-mouthing student only to get his tuition... and to keep her university job?"

I shot back, "Or fear because those students were getting ready to be deported. Administrators wanted to break down the instructors so they would go ahead and pass them. *She* was terrified because she didn't want any Saudis who paid for grades to come after *her*."

At this accusation, Agent Garrett stiffened and Agent Nelson widened his eyes, both agents trying *not* to give away any surprise at such a revealing statement.

Backing up my accusation, I said, "Grades are high stakes for them since they have to go home to face family after failing, and getting deported is so shameful for them since they are representing their country, and from what I understand, Saudi students are punished so severely if they fail – even if they can't do the work they are still whipped or killed – it still happens even if there is a legitimate reason they can't pass – like a learning disability."

Agent Garrett said, "I don't know about that."

"It's unfortunate but not every student is cut out to do university work.," I said. My eyes roamed the floor in search of anything else to add.

Agent Nelson said, "If this is an isolated incident, then there's not a lot for us to go on, but if there are any other incidents occur that threaten our *national security*, then we can do something about it. . . ."

I was flabbergasted as I pondered. Any other threats? Wasn't that enough? I couldn't believe what I was hearing. Does a person have to be half dead before any authorities take action?

I quickly retorted, "That's not the whole story. FBI needed to be alerted because of what Ms. Bryson told me before she became supervisor."

"What story is that?" said Agent Nelson.

Straightening up and contesting his lack-of-evidence excuse, I said, "She told me that there were students from Middle Eastern countries, Saudi students, who were *NOT* here to learn English --they have no future plans for classes in their major or to get a job – just here for no good."

Agent Nelson said innocently, "So *what* is their goal?"

Firmly emphasizing each word, I said, "She told me that they were here to learn about chemical engineering; to plan attacks in major metropolitan cities like D.C., Chicago, and even Cincinnati. Here to terrorize and kill Americans."

Sensing the agents were scrutinizing my every move and twitch, I was keenly aware of any flinch I made from head to toe. I was aware of anything that would unintentionally indicate that what I was saying was the truth. Feeling as if I was gesturing too much and realizing it, I put my hands in my lap and tried to keep still. Skeptical, they both looked at each other and looked back at me perplexed.

Questioning my accusations, Agent Garrett said, "Threatening students on a campus, in addition to their caseload, can be an ordeal for any campus police or administration to deal with, but we'll look into the incident."

The asperity and condescension in his voice bothered me because I felt like I had been written off. But on college campuses, violence seemed to be the norm, so I suppose that threats and terrorizing instructors was a simply a walk in the park.

With disdain, Agent Nelson remarked irritatingly, "Well, we don't know for sure if it's a strong indication of any future attack. We would know if there were any strange activities going on. . . large sums of chemicals being sold or students staying here with fraudulent visas, but that's for Homeland Security to deal with." His speaking was calm and collected.

Babbling, I went on, "But she told me that she knew who was at the head of this terrorist group and that he was working here to recruit students into the sleeper cell."

Sternly, Agent Nelson said, "What's his name?" "His name is Abdullah Alqahtani and he's an older man who was in several of my classes."

"Did he need to learn English?" asked Agent Garrett.

With an are-you-kidding-me tone, I said, "No, he knows English perfectly so there's no reason for him to be in the country. Ms. Bryson said that he was trying to brainwash students to get them into murdering as many Americans as possible." No matter what I said my accusations and assertions fell on deaf ears and that would be the end of it. I thought, "Hey, I'm the victim, why are they treating me like I did something wrong?" Solemnity. Except with shame for giving them busywork to have to deal with – and a guilt trip for saying anything.

With that, Agent Nelson asked me if there was anything else that I needed to tell them and make them aware of, and I told him that was it. Standing up, they took out their cards and after handing me the info, zipped up their coats. Investigation over. *Isn't a possible terrorist attack worth looking into? That just kept running through my mind and I couldn't shake it.*

Making their way to the door, Agent Nelson stopped when he saw a small, red, white and blue Romney-Ryan campaign sign used to rally a crowd leaning against a windowsill at the top of the steps. The sign was autographed by Ann Romney. It had in dark marked lines,

"To Madison, Ann Romney." In a different, friendlier voice, "Hey, look at that –it's signed by Ann Romney." He now obviously saw me in a different light, as a person who stood for what they believed in. Then he said, "Darn," and I said, "Yeah, darn is right."

CHAPTER THREE

After the agents left, I watched through my window as their car sped off and my eyes darted around the neighborhood to see if anyone had seen me with two official-looking men leaving my home. At this time of day, everyone had left for work or school. Scanning up and down the road, I didn't see a soul. *Whew, No one saw the agents enter or exit.* There was no one around that noticed --or so I thought, except the old lady who lived directly across the street, Janice. Janice was a thin-as-a-rail bony skeleton with frizzy red hair that looked like she had been messing with the electrical outlets too much. She kept tabs on everything and knew every person's schedule. If anyone deviated from their normal routine, she would be asking about it all right. When she got the lowdown on someone, she resembled a cat with a hump on its belly – the proverbial cat had swallowed a mouse. She had her flowery curtains pulled around her head and was watching the actions unfold like a mesmerized soap opera fan, earnestly desiring to see the next pivotal scene. Pulling the curtains shut, I overturned the edges and pulled the string to the blinds down as far as possible – all in an attempt to keep out busybodies, or anyone who would be gossiping about the men at my home.

Standing in the middle of the room, I was bewildered at how to answer questions from prying neighbors – but I couldn't worry about that now. Taking in that The FBI was actually in my home, I started to shiver and shake in a cold sweat. I couldn't stop hyperventilating –I remembered the anxiety medication that the doctor had given me. I scurried into the kitchen, rummaged through the cabinet and knocking over several other prescriptions, and I found the pills. Downing several and putting my head under the faucet to get a little water to force them down, my heart pounded with the audible beating. Swallowing and gulping the meds, hoping that would stave off another episode, I took my asthma inhaler and went and collapsed on the sofa, only to stare up at the ceiling in fright. It was morning but I was exhausted. For hours, I kept pondering what the outcome of this would be, but I knew that there would be a lot more questions before this was over. Did they believe me? Was I able to make any point about the seriousness of the threats? Were more Americans in danger with this potential threat? Would another attack happen here, on American soil? I couldn't speak. As much as I mistakenly believed that I had nixed my habit of relying on medication, the recent visit had brought back trauma of what happened to me and the what ifs had returned to me. What if someone came after me to hurt me? What if... and my thoughts kept spiraling in irrational thoughts. Fear really does stand for false events appearing real. The only thing I could do was to remind myself that God was in control and not to fear, but I just couldn't stop staring at the wall and wondering what if, what if there were another life lost because of terrorism … I had to have faith that it would work out, all in its own timing, and for good.

In my attempt to supply information to authorities, I felt like the person who was being apprehended. Yeah, I knew there would be a "surprise" at my door that day, but that wasn't the surprise that I anticipated... and what is the meaning of the word "surprise" anyway?

CHAPTER FOUR

A cool, crisp autumn day awakened the city of Cincinnati and outlying areas. Forest green grass was covered with a hard frost that settled like little Swarovski crystals dangling from an Austrian chandelier. The sun shone forth its warmth and was slowly melting away the frosty dew droplets, softening the tender ground into sublime moisture – moisture enriching the earth and ushering in a new season. Even people who loved summer would be appreciate this time of year as leaves displayed all varied colors of golden yellow, veridian green, and brick red. Groves of trees in the distant hilly areas yearned for visitors to escape and succumb to the beauty there – a place of refuge.

Wrapping my cotton scarf of royal blue and gold around my neck, I threw my bag and purse over my shoulder, set the house alarm, and slid on my clogs. Hoonnnkkk! Honnkkk!, honnkkk!! I jumped at the loud sound that seemed in the room with me. No doubt it was my colleague Maya whom I carpooled with to the bilingual school down the road from my home. I was only tutoring several days a week at the school which left me enough time to pursue hobbies. But my mind was on a murder and that was consuming my time when I wasn't at school. Even though the school was only five or six miles away, there was a drastic difference in the areas, the school being in the slums. I locked my front door and jumped into the small, sun-yellow VW bug. Maya, another teacher, always had a sour expression on her face and was never grateful to have a job in this city.

"Good morning," I chirped, pretending to be OK.

She gave me a half smile and said, "Yep, morning." Maya had been raised in Mexico City, and she had come to Ohio in order to build a new life from the poor conditions that she had in Monterrey, Mexico. She wore a gold bracelet and earrings, and her silk clothes made a swishing sound rubbing against her portly body. She tried to hide her accent, but when she got excited, her accent was more pronounced. She whisked the car down Westbrook Road and around a traffic circle onto Vista Road. I was reluctant to mention about being questioned, but I couldn't hide my nervousness as I looked around each corner as if we would be stopped and questioned. She could see out of the corner of her eye that I was unusually nervous.

Maya said, "Are you OK today? You seem a little frazzled."

"I'm fine. I just had a late night. And I had a dream that something bad was going to happen. I don't know what."

Maya said jokingly, "What kind of dream? Like we have to stay late and coach sports after school?"

"No, it was more like something along the lines of 9-11 But I can't put my finger on it. I saw smoke and people running."

Maya said, "Ooohhh, that sounds terrible." (which sounded like tereeble). "But that couldn't happen here."

"Why not? It could happen anywhere." I was defensive and ticked off that she was being naïve.

"Cincy is such a tiny place. There's nothing that happens here. Petty theft." I thought, What? Doesn't she watch the news or read about the drug busts and trafficking?

I said, "I think that you're being naïve. Hamilton County is the hotbed of terrorism. There's all kinds of things going on here – from heroin to plots to . ."

Knowing that I sounded dramatic, I lowered my head to look away. Maya gave a sarcastic shake of the head.

She said, "Speaking of terrorism, I did hear something about some Saudi students at UC last night. On the news, they said . . ."

Overreacting, I said, "Saudi students did what?"

Oblivious to my anxiousness, she calmly explained, "There was some sort of fire in one of the buildings on campus and a couple of Saudi students were seen running from the building."

"Was anyone hurt? Did they catch who did it?"

"No, I don't think so, but it is highly suspicious. The police are looking into it."

"See," I said, petulantly, "Those Saudis are up to no good. They could've killed so many people."

Maya said defensively, "They have to prove it. There are so many disgruntled students these days." I was in awe how she stood up for people who were on a rampage trying to maim or kill.

Finally, she pulled into a parking spot on the hill, overlooking the business and factories with smokestacks that shot the fog into the air, like towers reaching for heaven. But they were only man-made buildings that could tumble to the ground from any blast. I grabbed my bags as Maya locked up the car and I walked briskly to the entrance on the side to get to my classroom while she went in the front office entrance.

Barely muttering, "See ya later after school."

And she gave me a perfunctory, "Good day."

CHAPTER FIVE

December 2012

December 1st – Winter moves in and sets a chill on Cincinnati and outlying areas keeping it blanketed with snow. Dreary days drew on – A new season was grabbing hold of the city of Cincinnati with snow which blew in the cold accompanied with sullen feelings of cold months ahead. Winters in Cincinnati usually set upon the city besieging it with relentless cold and dampness – a dampness that never went away. Flurries swirled with backdrops of lavender skies that danced over the streets quickly retreating out of the city. Amid the foreboding skies, people managed to greet each other in perfunctory style.

Icicles hung over the protruding roof overlay and sprinkles of sunshine melted the melancholy of the season away. Drips of water left little indentations in the snow-covered bushes and people emerging from homes in bundled attire were out and about in the short winter day. There was an air of excitement and expectant joy leading up to the holidays – but it felt ominous too.

Waking up early, I heard my answering machine and my good friend saying, "Hey Maddie, this is Gretchen, do ya wanna go ice skating today or sometime this weekend?" Hearing her voice always made me feel better, though I didn't know if I cared about going all the way downtown to skate. We had known each other since our days in DC where we both got our graduate degrees from American University. Gretchen had family here and knew how to have fun in Cincinnati. She had family who had been here for years and had contacts. Since we were both single, we liked hanging out together and talking about our jobs and commiserating at times.

Dialing her number, I really couldn't decide if I wanted to go out or not. Braving the cold was not at all appealing to me. It was five degrees with wind chill of 10 below. Whistling and rustling with the clink-clink of the flag outside hitting the pole meant a cold night in the Tri-State.

Gretchen in her always upbeat way, asked, "Hey Maddie, ready for some skating this evening?

"Ugh, this evenin'? I dunno –I think I'm coming down with a cold and ..."

"What other excuse do you have for . . . ?"

"Oh, I'm just not in the mood to get all wet. It's so crowded with families this time of year..."

Persistently, Gretchen said, "But that's when it's fun to see all of the holiday decorations – it'll lift your spirits."

Begrudgingly, I said, "Oh, I guess it wouldn't kill me for a couple of hours."

"No, it wouldn't kill you. Be there at your place at 6."

"OK, I'll get my skates out," and hanging up, I thought, am I really in the mood for this? But there was no getting out of it now.

****

Later, I got out my big quilted coat, wool mittens, earmuffs, and big suede boots that were really too big so I wore two pairs of socks. The entire winter outfit must have weighed 15 pounds, or maybe it felt heavier because of the weight of setting my mind into having fun when I didn't feel like it. Ding dong. Another ring of the bell.

OK, OK, I'm coming, deciding to feign some holiday cheer. Opening the door, I saw Gretchen decked out in a holiday outfit and bubbly as ever. Gretchen was small with short, choppy, blonde hair, greenish eyes, and dimply cheeks that burst forth radiance. We were kindred spirits and she emanated constant energy. She was the epitome of enthusiasm and a carefree attitude. Gretchen's clothes almost made me laugh – her brick red cap woven with snowflakes, her short pants like German liederhosen, her striped red and green socks highlighting her pointy shoes – with her rosy cheeks, she resembled an elf.

"Ya ready to take off?"

In a deep, monotone voice, I said, "Yep, I suppose so."

We headed out to her car onto the side roads out of Fairfield and down I-75 toward Fountain Square near Sixth and Main Streets. Heading down the highway was easy since most drivers were on their way home out of the city, not towards downtown this time of day. We took the Main St. exit with our heads swinging back and forth in search of a parking space.

Gretchen said, "Oh gee, more people here than I thought... let's head farther down to the Collins Garage."

Turning into the parking garage, I had an urge to tell Gretchen to park on the street but we were bumper to bumper and people were eyeing spaces closest to the restaurants and cafes. Families were huddled in groups all eager to spend an evening at the square, seeing a movie, standing in front of a marquee sign, or shop in one of the stores along the row. Traipsing down to the rotund ice rink, I saw people who were seated and lacing up shoes and parents who were drinking the hot chocolate and relaxing and watching their kids. Gretchen burst onto the ice like a pro ice skater and I eased my way on embarrassingly clinging to the handrail and inching forward. Gretchen swung by me and I could feel the breeze from her zooming past me, all with an elated posture.

"Isn't this terrific?"

I faked a smile and nodded. While Gretchen danced around the rink like a ballerina in an Austrian opera, I was admiring the couples skating side by side and holding interlocked arms – I admitted to myself that I was a little envious of those couples, but had to make the best of this. Feigning fun was not in my repertoire with friends. Gretchen was fun, and I didn't want to ruin her night with a bummed attitude. Skating with an intense speed, I managed to catch up to Gretchen who was in a world of her own and loving every minute of it. We skated for another hour or so pointing out the decorations and lights that were being turned on at dusk and hearing the oohing and ahhing of people who were also taking notice of the bright and impressive oversized wreaths. Blinking multi-colored lights reflected onto a silver and gold tinseled tree and ornaments.

With flushed rosy cheeks and huffing to catch her breath, I said, "About ready to call it an evening?"

"*You're* tired? Yeah, I'm about done too . . . but let's get something to eat on the way. . . . I'm starved."

Finding a vacant bench off to the side of the rink, we sat down, took off our skates, and stuffed them in our bags. We rushed back to the car like two kids released from school. Throwing our skates in the backseat, we zoomed down the curved exit ramp, paid the parking fee and rolled back out onto the busy street –bumper to bumper as far as one could see to the next stop light. We headed up Elm St. and onto Central Parkway. Once on I-75, we could make some good time back home. Or so we assumed that we'd be back home in nothing flat.

Out of nowhere, *sreeeeecchhhing, swoosh, zooom.* Deafeningly loud sirens, flashing police car lights, and unmarked rescue vehicles sped by us up Clay St. toward the university. As we got closer to the university area, we noticed that stop lights were out. Homes and businesses, deserted. Onyx black windows and people locking their doors. A few people were congregating outside on the sidewalk toward lamp posts. The dull amber light shone on their leather jackets and their heads darting around looking for an explanation. A young mother with two small children in ragged clothes had a flashlight in one hand and her two children were hanging on her side as a young cub tries to bury itself in a bear's warm arms. Gretchen stepped on the gas, and the force of turning sharp curves made my body sway back and forth. What was going on? I turned on the radio because of the blaring sirens. A loud beeping sound from a university station announced, "Due to a loss of power, all evening classes, I repeat, all evening classes will be canceled. This is an emergency situation. I repeat, This is an emergency situation. Please take precautions and remain inside until further notice."

A young male voice said, "If you are on campus, please go immediately to your dormitory and lock all doors. If someone is expecting you, call to let them know you are safe. Get to some place that you are safe and please heed our warnings."

Another female voice started talking, but I turned the sound down.

Angling toward the right side of the road, Gretchen roughly maneuvered the car over to the right to allow the emergency vehicles to pass.

"Guess another fire around campus," Gretchen said as she pulled the car back into the flow of traffic.

"I dunno, looks pretty serious... maybe another drug raid . . . *Not* the best area of the city."

Staring at the cars with full attention, Gretchen said, "Yep. Probably a drug bust." Now I was really anxious to escape this mess and get home.

Relief as we got back to my neighborhood. Stopping at Panera's we picked up some food and got back to my place. It only took another hour or so, but we made it. Pulling into my driveway, the air was so cold that mists were seeping up from the ground and there were ice crystals forming on the inside of my glass panes. Changing into dry clothes, we scarfed down our sandwiches and soup and watched ice skating competitions.

An hour or so later, Gretchen said, "You know, I'm kinda feelin' wiped out. Mind if I take off?"

"Nah, I'm ready to hit the hay myself."

She got her stuff together and left with barely audible, "Call ya tomorrow." And I crawled into bed, ready to call it a day.

CHAPTER SIX

Creating a ruckus of noise, the pesky birds outside my window woke me and a new day sprang forth. Stretching out my legs, I could feel the soreness from the skating the day before. There was a twinge of pain in my shoulder and arm as I turned over in bed. Waiting until the annoying leg cramp subsided, I finally got up to fix a cup of tea. I turned on the TV in the living room and waiting for the water to boil, I looked over my calendar and started marking the calendar for appointments that I had stored on my phone. The usual TV ads for carpet cleaning and hair replacement were showing when a local female newscaster appeared on the UC campus. She was bundled in a down feather, sea blue ski jacket and cap and she clutched her microphone in one hand and pushed the ear piece farther into her ear, straining to receive word when to begin.

She turned toward the camera man and said, "Yes, this is just in. We have breaking news from the University of Cincinnati campus. We have a report of a murder on campus. Apparently, this murder happened yesterday evening. Investigators are determining the specifics but they are moving frantically to get as much information as they can."

On the left of the screen, a broadcaster for WGNN, Barry Bosner, in the main TV station said, "Excuse me, Megan, do we know when this murder took place?"

Megan said, "We're not exactly certain the exact time, but we're speculating that it was sometime later in the evening. It's so early in the investigation . . ."

Barry interrupted, "What can you tell us about the victim. Male or female?

Student or professor?"

Completely stunned. I now realized that the commotion that Gretchen and I encountered on the way home was from the police responding to the murder the previous evening. My mind went blank as the words continued as background mumbles and the questioning continued.

Megan said, "We have a 40-ish female, mid 40s who appears to be the apparent victim of a brutal homicide. Geisler Hall."

Oh, I thought, Geisler Hall, that's where I taught. Losing focus of my hands, I spilled the boiling tea and dropped the cup onto the floor with a splash about six inches in front of the TV . . . staring blankly into the TV, I watched the details emerge. Turning up the TV, the volume hit the walls in a loud pitch.

The broadcaster continued. "We have a female victim who was apparently an administrator... Hold on, I'm getting more information (as he holds his earpiece closer)... Hearing the word "administrator," my heart starts pounding. "The victim appears to be a Loretta Breeson," as he stumbles over her last name, "I'm sorry, that's Bryson. The police have roped off the area for no access until they can take evidence from the scene. They do tell me that they are suspicious of anyone who may have been in that building at that time, so they are interviewing or anyone who may have information. We'll bring you more details as they become available.. ."

Running to the bathroom, I went to the sink and turn on the water and splash water on my face. Looking at myself in the mirror, I wondered, How did this happen?

Who did this? A weird surreal feeling rushed over me, and sweating profusely, I slowly keeled over on the floor in a fetal position. Drops hit the floor in little splashes. Clutching the bathroom vanity, I held on as my head darted back and forth. I didn't know how long it was, but I stared straight ahead in shock. After getting enough strength, I leaned over and pulled a towel off a rack and wiped my entire face and arms of sweat even though my limbs felt cold to the touch. Speechless, I went to the sofa and clutched the remote control, started abruptly changing channels from one local station to another, watching how all of the TV stations were reporting on the murder.

WHGP showed another reporter on another side of the campus reporting the murder.

The caption below read, "UC Administrator Murdered." A young blonde female broadcaster bundled up in the cold, reports, "The police are looking at several students who may have been running from the building and whether or not they can get any pictures from surveillance cameras. The murder happened around 8:55 taken from the camera and the police are studying it carefully to find out who perpetrated this horrific crime. Unfortunately, the power went out . . ." News continued, and I wiped my cold and clammy hands on my pajamas and gulped down the tea, my mouth dry and my body dehydrated.

Throwing on my jeans and sweater, I turned on the computer and scanned images the local newspaper displayed of the scene and what details the police were giving the public. Every local station was reporting on the homicide. A large, boldfaced headline in the Cincinnati Enquirer caught my eye:

CINCINNATI, OH – December 13, 2012. A brutal murder happened on the campus of the University of Cincinnati between 7 and 8 pm in Geisler Hall. The victim is 44-year-old Loretta Bryson Academic Dean in charge of international students. It appears that Ms. Bryson was struck on the head with a blunt object and was found lying over her desk. She struggled to call 9-1-1 but wasn't able to complete the call. As it appears, Ms. Bryon died before she could get help. The crime scene is horrific as blood is splattered on all parts of her office. The police have no suspects at this time, but they are investigating any possible leads. No one is allowed in this building where evidence is being taken. Students who have class in this building are being directed by campus officials to other buildings and rooms on campus. Police are warning all students to be extremely careful so please heed those warnings." And the broadcaster goes on about details as I sit. Numb.

I saw the slide show pictures with crimson blood everywhere …. It's oozing and splattered in an abstract modern art design. I was sickened by the sight of it.

CHAPTER SEVEN

Flipping open my laptop, I scrolled down through the pictures. Click. Picture 1. The outside of the building was a winding sidewalk and two double doors, a large sign to the right that says Geisler Hall, and students in groups holding their backpacks and standing in awe. Their faces were like stone and their bodies captured in time – mannequins without the ability to show emotion. Chilling. I brace for the next photo.

Click. Picture 2. The hallway leading up to the murder scene. displaying posters of faraway places and student posters on ivory, cinder block walls. The blue tinted overhead fluorescent lights were sterile and the nubby marine blue carpet shows a detective caught kneeling and removing some evidence from a piece of the molding jutting out from the side wall. Reality of what happened has set it.

Click. Picture 3. The office where Loretta was murdered. Even though the body was removed, there was a puddle of blood on the desk and dripping over the side onto the floor. Goopy brick red blood – a gel-like consistency. I scrutinized every picture to see any little thing that looks out of place. Splattered on the walls and on the floor, the blood was everywhere.

Desperate for air, I slid open the balcony door to go out to catch my breath. Leaning over the side, I swooned back and forth at the sight of the pavement below. I'm in the kitchen again and downing sedatives with lots of water. I couldn't help it but I know that I'm hooked on them again, but who cares? This is too much for me now.

No words to describe the murder. My eyes are seeing but my brain cannot capture the image – my conscious mind was like a gatekeeper that will only allow in the picture of what it wants and can accept into reality – and it's rejecting this. Horrific and Incomprehensible.

The rest of the evening I wondered how someone broke into the building and murdered and escaped. It's 2 am, and unable to sleep, I went outside to sit underneath a sky. Yanked into this horrific event, I was consumed by this. I was now in a world that presupposes that space separates us from God and from each other – only an illusion since according to science we are all connected – entangled in a web that we spin creating our lives and own destiny. But now detached.

Around 3 am, I laid down on my bed and dozed from sheer exhaustion, waking every 10 minutes or so at the slightest sounds. Outside, life goes on with 20-somethings getting home from a party or the nurse next door ending her hospital shift. Every time my head dropped off to momentary sleep, it jolted me awake with eyes wide open from interrupted, fearful dreams – like the familiar falling-and-catching-yourself dream. Thank God, though, that we awaken and realize that we didn't succumb to hitting of the ground and the ensuing heart attack. After hearing my heart pound outside my chest, I was more content to wear myself out with the insomnia.

****

In the morning, the sun broke through a nebulous, charcoal blanket of clouds that spewed forth a gloomy day. Little pellets of ice pinged the windows and covered the roads leading to ominous travel warnings and treacherous roads all across Cincinnati. The investigation of Loretta's murder was hampered by the weather and dominated by news of collisions on I-71 and 75. I changed the TV channels in rapidly looking for any more updates. Only a two-minute clip of students on campus. Two Asian students, a petite female student and a tall, languid male, both with taciturn expressions, slouch over in front of the bear cat statue.

Frances Burchetti, local reporter for ABC Channel 9, interviews some Korean students. "Excuse me, are you two students here on campus?"

The students shook their heads yes.

Frances continues, "How are the students feeling about a murder happening right here on campus? And what are the students doing to exercise caution from a killer that could be right here on campus?"

The female student looked down waiting for her friend to answer.

A tall, slender male Korean student says with an accent, "We are first-year students here from Korea and we are scared but crime is everywhere. We walk together and don't go any place without someone. That is a good rule."

Frances said matter-of-factly, "What are other students saying about this horrific crime?"

With contorted face, the student responded, "We know our classmates, they are afraid, but we have to live our lives. Stuff happens everywhere."

Turning to the camera, Frances tells viewers, "That's what the UC campus is dealing with as well as campus police who are patrolling the campus. Fear is palpable but students are going about their daily routines the bet they can. Back to you in the studio...."

Over the next few days, all of the national TV stations were airing the tragic murder on campus and offer no explanation for the event. To me, they glossed over the whole murder, just another event. It gave me pause to think of all of the other unsolved murders that news stations report. People are unconcerned until a murder happens in their backyard.... and it does happen in every part of a city from the inner city to the suburbs to the country. . . . and I turned off the TV.

CHAPTER EIGHT

Days go by and I have little contact with anyone. Getting through the day and trying to look for work was overwhelming – plus, I had the nagging feeling that the FBI would be back eventually to question me. Occasionally, I called an old friend in Fayetteville, NC who is a Methodist minister who talks to me in a grandfatherly way. Fayetteville, NC is a small Army town where no one really desires to be stationed so alcohol and drug abuse as well as the frequent domestic abuse is common. Reverend Frank Freeman was a quiet man in his late 60s. His calming ways helped me to put things in perspective, and he always knew the right thing to say to help get me back in a positive mood or at least the energy to get up in the morning.

A secretary with a Southern drawl answered. "This is Southern Methodist Church. How may I help you?"

"I'd like to speak to Reverend Freeman, if possible."

"Hold on, dear. Let me put you through." After I minute, I hear Reverend Freeman.

"Hi, Reverend Freeman. This is Madison Hauck. I needed to talk to you.

"Well, Maddie, how're things going up there in Ohio?" Reverend Freeman said cordially.

In a solemn and low tone as someone in a funeral home, I said, "Did you hear about the murder on the UC campus?"

"Um, I've been out visiting so many of my parishioners that I'm not rightly sure if I know exactly ..." My voice, cracking and shaking, "There was a murder on the campus of the University of Cincinnati and the woman who was killed was, was my former supervisor."

There was total silence as Reverend Freeman was obviously searching for words of comfort.

"Oh Maddie, I'm so sorry to hear that. You must be devastated. Has anyone questioned you yet?"

Not wanting to go into the whole story over the phone, I simply said, "I told the authorities everything I knew about possible suspects."

"Then that's all you can do for now. They're probably working a lot more hours on it than you realize. You'll eventually hear something and it'll come to a conclusion." Rather relieved that someone knew about what what happening to me, I sighed.

"Concerned, Reverend Freeman continued, "Have you found any potential, full-time jobs?"

"No, finding work is fairly tough now," I said dejected.

"Well, don't give up. There's a job for you. You just haven't found it."

Reverend Freeman ends with his reassuring, "I know and God loves you." Suddenly, my problems didn't seem so big and that I still had an ounce of will to live. He had a knack for giving me a feeling that he knew exactly what I was going through and he had a smile in his voice – and I liked that a lot.

CHAPTER NINE

Two days before Christmas I was still oblivious to the fact that it was the holidays. Pictures for toys, clothes, jewelry and trinkets padded the pages of The Cincinnati Enquirer, and the stack of advertisements in the mail. Every Sunday morning after picking up the paper at my door I scanned for sales and what's new at Macy's. Today when I tipped over the bag to empty all of the paper and contents, it made a ka-thump as all of the paper landed in the middle of the floor. Sifting through the pile, I saw the retailer's all had holiday ads – RUSH – LAST CHANCE BEFORE XMAS SALE insert with children and adults of every age sporting clothes, bikes, and tech equipment. On page 9, there were only several lines about the murder. It read: Murder of Administrator at University of Cincinnati-- Investigation is into the murder of Loretta Bryson is ongoing. Evidence has not led police to any suspects at this time. Cincinnati Police will continue to interview anyone who might know something but there have been no developments to report." And that was it. While sifting through the local news for any information about local happenings, my phone rang. I heard the familiar sound of my brother, Chad. In his fifties, Chad with his soft gray hair, wavy and pushed back like a gardner who had been laboring outside. He and his wife spent all of their time at a Pentecostal church north of Charlottesville, VA in Earlysville where he spent his days ministering to people. Earlysville was a small town where the local wealthy built their two-story brick homes and avoided city life where University of Virginia graduates bragged about their children matriculating in UVA and carrying on the family history or pursuing law, medicine, or another graduate program. To the elite professional, Charlottesville was the ideal big-picture place where the biggest delights are country club golfing and getting your picture in the paper holding some kind of trophy or award – in other words, you have to be somebody to fit in there. Chad had always resented anything or anyone that had to do with getting ahead in the world and it baffled me why he resided so close to a good ol' boy city with generational wealth – any person with money, to him, was seen as a snob and therefore made excuses for being an insurance salesman who gave free "counseling" to anyone who found himself at the lowest point their life.

Hey girl, what's been happen' in the queen city?"

Feeling a little lift from hearing his voice, I said, "Nothin'. Whatcha been up to in Earlysville?"

Exhausted, he said, "Gettin' my schedule back from taking the young adults at church to Tianchang, China."

"That must have been rough – trying to teach children about God who can't even speak English."

Chad said, "Oh, they're learning. It just takes time to get them up to speed with English so we just love on them. And they look forward to the toys and gifts we take 'em."

"Don't they have dirty water there? What do you drink?"

Chad said, "Yeah, the water is dirty but we drink it anyway." For that, I had to give him kudos and respect because he was a better person than I for going to such a an unsanitary place.

He said, "Are you teaching now?"

Subdued, I said, "I'm OK – just looking for new full-time teaching jobs."

"You're looking for new teaching ...?" "Yeah, please don't ask. The last job just didn't work out – a mess down there in the city."

"Well, sometimes it's best to get away and get your mind off your troubles. If you want to spend some time with Maribeth and me, you're welcome to come to our house.

"I said, "Uh, I don't know, I've had so much going on here." "It's just a thought."

Maribeth was Chad's wife and she was a nurse at the UVA Hospital where she had worked for over 30 years. Not having children, she lavished all of her affection and love on the children at her church who she called "God's chil-ren," omitting the "d" as Southerners sometimes do.

Aware that Chad was talking to me, Maribeth took the phone from him and said excitedly, "I'm making my famous red velvet cake and peach and blueberry cobbler."

Apologizing, I said, "I'm not big on sweets."

"If sweets aren't for ya, we've got plenty of other good dishes –lamb, honeyed ham, biscuits, and those yummy green beans." Anytime I thought about food, I could feel my mouth start oozing forth saliva.

Somewhat skiddish about making the trip, I said, "You've sold me with the menu. I'll be there tomorrow around 5 pm for Christmas Eve service."

Maribeth was tickled pink. "Great. I'll get your room ready."

CHAPTER TEN

Driving to Virginia is one spectacular journey, especially through West Virginia where scenic views take one's breath away atop peaceful overlooks that scan as far as the eye can see. Even though I was a Virginian at heart, this state had the most incredible views, and I had to stop at the lookouts to see God's grand landscape. After paying the toll, I drove down one long mountain and taking some turns on a curvy highway with wide, steel guardrails, found a place to take a break. I took a break on a circular, cement area with a scope to insert coins and see far into the distance. Tourists and motorists pulled over and they can see rolling hills with viridian green trees, all perfectly planted in a lush sweep of trees that is like a piece of green velvet laid in flowing ripples across the countryside. I took deep breaths to gear up for the last leg of my trip to Earlysville. There was no greater pleasure than taking in the nature all around us. After sipping some iced tea and eating some crackers, I drive on and see the *Welcome to Virginia* visitors sign. After several hours and going over another mountain, I took the 29 north exit to Earlysville. After passing the stores on 29, I arrived at my brother's and sister-in-law's house as the sun began to set across Blue Ridge. On their front steps, Chad and Maribeth were shivering as Chad was drinking hot chocolate from a Christmas mug and Melinda in her holiday sweater clutched her arms touching her elbows in an obvious chill.

"How was the drive?" said Chad.

Cold and fatigued, I said, "Oh pretty good, long but the scenery is always magnificent."

"Let's get you unpacked so you can rest." Chad grabbed my suitcase and bags and takes them up the steps to the guest bedroom, a room with a frilly, flowery bed and little knick-knacks with sayings of holiday cheer.

As we all enter the house, Maribeth said, "You must be starved. Let me fix you some Brunswick stew." Brunswick stew is a Virginian stew with pork, chicken, and vegetables and is very hearty in cold weather.

Sighing I said, "Um, I'm a little tired out from the drive. I don't want to impose on you. A sandwich is fine."

Chad said, "Oh. That's Maribeth's fun – cooking for people and lookin' out for 'em."

"OK, if she doesn't mind, then I'll take some stew."

Maribeth scurried off to the kitchen to prepare some fine homecookin' or what they call "vittles" down South. Cooking made her happier than a honeybee in a sweet rose.

Chad and Maribeth's house was simple and hints of Christian décor with figurines and embroidered hangings that filling the room. I plopped down in the recliner and Chad sat on the sofa, upright as if ready to interview someone. I could read hesitancy in Chad's face.

He said, "How are ya really getting' along these days? You don't seem like yourself."

"It's going OK. I'm just dealing with a lot from what happened down at UC... the murder of my former boss." My voice was almost whimpering. I added, "And I dunno what the police are thinking. They questioned me about the harassment from Saudi students who were upset at her mismanagement... I dunno if they'll ever find..."

Chad stopped my pity party, "Oh Maddie, they'll find out who did it – it takes time but my daughter Lizzie is a forensic pathologist and they can find evidence that you would not believe."

With several tears welling in my eyes, I said, "I hope so 'cause there's a murderer out there who could kill someone else."

Reassuring me in a lower voice, Chad said, "We saw that on the national news and it is a huge story. It just takes time but it'll resolve itself, God will see to it. We'll pray over it."

Suddenly, I felt as though a storm had quelled into a tranquil oasis where I could lie down with all worries wiped clean and clear. Feeling a hunger pang and smelling the aroma from the kitchen, I sat at their mission-style style dining set on a bench with cloth napkins and chowed down on the chunky stew, grilled cheese, and succulent bread pudding, washing it down with sweet tea that had so much sugar it ran like syrup on glass rim. Chad and Maribeth went to the Christmas Eve service while I stayed home and unpacked. Feeling sluggish from the sumptuous meal, I collapsed and drifted off into a deep sleep– a sleep unlike any that I'd had in weeks. Outside, the mist settled slowly down on a nearby pond and winter's barren pine trees stood dormant in the stark cold – and it slept on until the coming spring.

****

Upon waking to Christmas the next morning, I smelled French toast and coffee downstairs. I wanted to lie in bed all day but knew that there would be Christmas festivities. Buttoning up my flannel pajamas and slipping on velvety slippers, I took one step at a time down the creaky steps as a child spying on parents putting out

Christmas gifts. Chad and Maribeth were talking on the phone wishing cousins, relatives, and friends a Merry Xmas and preparing for several parishioners to come over for holiday dinner.

"Merry Christmas," belted out Chad.

Slowly descending the steps, I said, "Merry Christmas," and gave them both a bear hug. They were distributing gifts and the few small gifts that I put under the tree last night seemed minute compared to the oversized boxes tied with large glittery ribbons that Chad had pulled out from underneath the tree adorned with lights of every color flashing randomly. Chad and Maribeth exchanged gifts of jewelry and perfume and Max Lucado books.

Maribeth said, "Mercy, you were sooo thoughtful."

Chad and then opened my gift, a book that a friend wrote about living spiritual lives and said, "Thank you."

They gave me a calendar with inspirational quotes and with the hoopla of Christmas morning over, the holiday for me had built up with such excitement that always left me with a somewhat strange letdown. The crinkled wrapping paper was stacked in balls and empty China plates with leftover morsels were stacked in the sink and on the counters. Their cat, a Siamese, named Blinky, buried under a stack, peered out with its dark, frightful almond eyes. Always in the back of my mind, I was wondering about Loretta's murder case, wondering how long it would be before the outcome – always on edge about another horrific news story, another crime. And when I listened to the Christmas pastors on TV, I zoned out in front of the TV. Parades, festivities, and funny ads but I sat expressionless, unable to concentrate. What were the FBI, police, and families doing to solve this case? Were they working on the case at this time or did they put it off until after the New Year? Were they examining any evidence? Did they have a suspect list? I couldn't let it go.

****

When soft snowflakes settle on box bushes, and birds begin to hush in evening's arrival, the beginning of a cold and blustery night billows in. Outside, ashen and mystical objects lay under gray skies. I retreated to the spare bedroom upstairs and pulled up recent internet articles on the murder investigation. Not wanting anyone to see what I was doing, I was keenly aware of Maribeth or Chad wandering in and startling me, so I kept glancing back in anticipation of a voice causing me to jump, jolting me from my own private investigation. I entered every word in the search window that I could think of – UC murder, unsolved crimes on UC campus, and Loretta Bryson – but none of the searches turned up any new information. I could hear Chad and Maribeth in the other bedroom getting dressed for dinner and Maribeth saying, "Do these earrings go with my outfit? Shouldn't I iron that shirt for you?" Chad mumbled in the background. Still distracted by my incessant curiosity, I still sat in jeans, turtleneck, and thick, itchy, nubby wool socks, entering searches and surmising that there was nothing new that the media could find and report on. I glanced at the clock, noticed that it was already 5:58 p.m. and with guests arriving soon, I changed quickly into a shimmery, black skirt, red laced blouse and put on dangling pearl earrings. Just in time. The guests were ringing the doorbell and entering with homemade cookies wrapped in Christmas paper and bows, poinsettias, and yellow boxes of candy. Maribeth, not missing a beat, was serving sausage balls, pieces of melon wrapped in prosciutto, and apple cider. A glass of wine would have been a good compliment to the appetizers but Maribeth and Chad didn't approve of alcohol, or what they called "the devil's drink," never mind any potential benefits from drinking beer or wine. I checked my appearance in the mirror and walked stiffly in high heels down the wooden steps to see half a dozen people meandering around the room, all looking as if they were salivating for a big dinner. With all of the decorations, I felt sentimental for my childhood and wondered where all of the joyous days went.

There was a lot of hugging, merriment, and laughter, and I hesitantly approached a couple eating the hors d'oeuvres.

A robust, stout man with rosy cheeks and a paunchy belly said, "Hi, I'm Kerry and this is my wife Cynthia." Cynthia was short, hunched over, and her small, round face was sallow and wrinkled. She looked tired and overworked.

She said, "Are you part of Chad's or Maribeth's family?"

"Yes, I'm Chad's sister, and I'm visiting for a few days from Ohio," while secretly dreading any questions as seemingly intrusive.

Kerry said, "Oh, we have relatives in Cleveland, and we like going out to the Midwest – there's something different about that area. There are a lot of people who are of German descent."

"Yeah, there are quite a few Germans who settled in the Ohio River area. Apparently, the river resembles the Rhine River in Germany so many years ago they planted themselves there because it reminded them of home."

The couple looked at each other and said, "Um, we've always wanted to go to Germany," and they saw another family that they wanted to talk to.

Kerry said, "Well, it was nice to meet you," and he stepped closer to another couple engaged in chit-chat. Teetering in my high heels, I sat down on the sofa, wishing that dinner was going to be served soon so I wouldn't have to make small talk. Several minutes later, a tall, languid man emerged from behind the people and sat down next to me. His friendly smile was ingratiating and he could somehow discern that I was feeling a little out of place. He wore faded green khakis, a wrinkled shirt with an indigo ink mark on the left pocket, a skinny, red, knit tie that dated back to the 1980s, and tousled, black curly hair with horn rim glasses. Anyone could peg him for an educator with his scruffy appearance.

He turned to me and shyly said, "Hi, My name is Alan and I am an assistant in the theology department at UVA. Maribeth and Chad certainly are two of the most hospitable people I know –always busy with doin' good --they've helped and shared what they have with others, and. . ."

"Yeah, they are giving people. They just know how to appeal to people who really need help," and squinting his clear onyx eyes asked, "And what's your name and what do you do? I bet you take care of children, I can see a caring spirit in you," slightly grinning and wanting me to open up.

"I'm Maddie and I," stammering, "I teach English at a school in Cincinnati," with a decline in tone.

Inquisitive, he said, "Why so blue and upset at this time of the year?" "Well, I used to have a more prestigious job so I'm kinda lookin to..."

"Used to? What does that mean?"

Realizing that I opened up a can of worms, I explained, "Well, I used to teach in Cincinnati but there were so many problems, problems with threatening students, cheating scandals with instructors, and ...."

Trying to tell about Loretta's murder, I cleared my voice and it was as if the words got stuck in my throat – I didn't care to go into it, not with a stranger and not at a party.

Alan's eyebrows rose in concern, and compassion emanated from his quiet demeanor.

"Well, Maddie, I can tell that you did whatever you had to do in that situation. God gives us situations that test our faith and doing the right thing is always seen by God."

Mentioning my name made me more comfortable with him. He comforted me so I was not as annoyed with his prying questions.

"God gives us two ways to go after death. There are the masses who go through the wide gate which is the gate that *most* go through and it is easy to pass through because we don't change in this life – and then there is the *narrow* gate and it is tougher to get through. But by *realization* and *recognition,* we strive to go through the narrow gate." He then smiled and said apologetically, "I'm sorry. You don't need a sermon at a Christmas dinner."

But I secretly wished that he could keep talking. "*Going through the narrow gate*"... what did that mean? Did I want to be like the masses that only go through the wide gate – who spend their lives thinking that life is just trying to make it and there is no way to change and adopt new ways of thinking, new ways of believing and new ways of acting. And how do we choose the right things? I only knew that this concept was intriguing to me, and I had to give some serious thought to the meaning of what he was saying to understand. Realizing and recognizing what life was all about was alluring and appealing to me.

Among the groups of guests in the living room, I saw several young teenagers seated on the cheap, folding chairs along the wall near the Christmas tree as Maribeth announced that dinner was ready. When Chad announced that dinner was ready, we all got up slowly, took the seats where Maribeth set for us, and ate a delicious dinner of roast turkey and ham with green beans, sweet potatoes, and rolls. To finish off the meal, I gorged on pies of every kind. And later that night, the meaning of "*going through the narrow gate*" kept replaying in my mind until I drifted off to a fretful slumber.

CHAPTER ELEVEN

Early the next morning, after a food hangover left me overstuffed and sluggish, I took a walk around the neighborhood to get some fresh air and decided what I could do in this predicament of finding Loretta's murderer. Putting on several sweaters and my coat, I felt hemmed in and almost not able to move all bundled up. Venturing out into the neighborhood, I slid down the steps and onto the slick road where split-level homes and large fenced-in yards ended in a cul-de-sac. Several dogs ran up to the edge of the fence and barked ferociously to warn of a stranger in the neighborhood. Startled and slipping on the asphalt, I fell down only to get up quickly (oblivious to being hurt or not) ignoring if I had been hurt. Even though I was wearing my all weather, fur-lined boots with two-inch treads, I hastily moved down the embankment, albeit falling which was sure to leave a few bruises on my knees and behind. Maple and poplar trees sagged with the ice bearing down on branches like burdensome problems weighing on weak shoulders. Icicles were pointing treacherously down like cave stalactites ready to break loose and fall onto some poor soul in some kind of dramatic ending to a medieval play. Making my way back to the house and attempting to avoid sliding off into the road made me hyper-aware of the weather dangers lurking around me. Pulling myself with the metal handrail into the house, I became resolute in solving Loretta's murder. Taking action was the only way. I wanted to be back home now and face reality and what I was compelled to do.

At the door, I tapped my boots against the front steps to get the ice off and left them at the front door. Inside it was toasty warm and I could see my face which was splotchy red and white from the exercise. I hung up my scarf and coat and shimmied into a small corner chair at the table covered with oatmeal, frothy, organic milk in a pitcher, and strawberries covered with cream. Not craving anymore food, I craved some high protein food to get some energy. I believe that speaking to a private detective would give me some insight in how to solve this murder. I needed to at least explore what I could do to find someone, a private detective, who had the same strong intentions in solving this murder. Searching the internet for private detectives in Cincinnati was no easy feat. I scrolled down lists and lists of investigators – and how to get a reference for a reputable investigator? There were agencies and individuals and some of the agencies were as far away as Dayton and Columbus. After perusing the list, I scribbled down my proposal to write a prospective detective. The search narrowed to about a dozen or so possible detectives that I could email – and a prompt response was always a good sign that the person was interested and serious about going forward with an investigation. I read the privacy agreement for all of the detectives.

I typed, "I desperately need a Private detective to look into the evidence of a murder. The police might suspect me in this case – need to clear my name. Need someone to examine the evidence. Please contact me to discuss this case."

I sent the email out with my cell phone number – whoever the first few people to answer would be at the top of my list to hire. Hours had gotten away from me and I laid down on the bed to rest.

Chad knocked on the door and said, "Are you sleeping the whole day?"

Getting up and opening the door, I groggily said, "Yep, doin' fine, but need to take care of some business."

"We know that what you're up against has gotta be difficult, so let us know if you need us to help in any way."

For some reason, I felt on the verge of tears, and I hugged him and said, "Thanks but I'm gonna be fine... once I find out the answers... and there's always a reason and explanation for everything."

Chad, pastorally said, "We'll keep praying there is a resolution to your problem and soon." I resumed my nap on the bed and not knowing how long I was asleep woke up sweating in a dark room with my phone ringing... I was blinking and disoriented. What time was it? In a half-sleep state, I grabbed my phone and on the display was "513 No Name" – a blocked number from Cincinnati.

****

With a raspy and barely audible voice, I said a faint, "Hello," and heard a friendly male voice. "Hello, may I speak to a Madison Hauck?"

Realizing that this was probably a detective in response to my emails, I pushed back the comforter, swept the hair from my face, and scrambled to find a pad and pen to take down notes.

"Yes, this is she."

"Ms. Hauck, this is Mike Singleton, and I am an investigator here in Cincinnati, and I received your email about assisting the police with the murder investigation of Loretta Bryson. Before I can assist you, I need to ask you some questions."

"Ask me whatever you need to know."

"I need to know why you are interested in the Loretta Bryon case and solving it?"

"I might be considered a suspect and I want to know if a Saudi student was responsible for it. Everything that I witnessed points to an angry student who wanted revenge."

Mike said, "Uh, well. . . ."

And I continued. "I think that the Cincinnati Police Department, campus police, and FBI need some assistance. I quit teaching there because I was threatened, harassed, and bullied."

"Sounds like pretty unfavorable working conditions."

Unnerved, I said, "Yeah, I'll say it was unworkable. I need to be able to defend myself in case I am made a suspect."

"I heard about this case in the news, and I can tell you that without even knowing the details that the police have a lot of interviewing to do, and if you haven't been questioned yet, then you probably aren't a suspect."

I repeated, "Aren't a suspect?"

"That's correct. Are not a suspect." I was getting worked up and entering defense mode. Sternly, I said, "Loretta Bryson was the gatekeeper for who could go on with their English studies here and if they didn't pass – many Saudi students were deported – she had to give them the bad news that they had to return to their home country.. Someone told me they were tortured when they got back to their home country. . . ."

Mike asked, "So if they couldn't make the grade then they were tortured?"

"Yep, they got beat or killed, but I do know that there was some severe punishment for not passing."

"Yeah, you might be right about that. Sounds like a nasty situation if you are the one responsible for sending them home."

"I would tell you more of the story but not over the phone. Do you think that you can help me?"

"Let me think. . . For me to get a better handle on exactly what I'm dealing with, send me a page stating the facts as you know them." I have 15 years' experience in tracking criminals, all kinds of cases. First, I have to tell you my rate and send you the agreement for any other expenses that I incur."

"What is your rate?" "I charge $75 per hour which is average and for any other expenses that I incur to help with the case."

"Send me the agreement because I'd like to hire you." "I have your email and you can fax it to me ASAP."

"I'll get it done today."

"Oh, Maddie, besides sending me the fact sheet, the first thing that I'll need to do to help with this case is to find out how amenable the police are to my assisting in this case."

"Yeah, right, will you solve who killed Loretta?"

"Ma'am, I'm sure gonna find out. I'm relentless with any case."

"Thanks so much," and hung up. The word "*relentless*" stuck with me throughout the next few days like a ferocious dog angrily holding onto a precious blanket.... and that blanket was my peace of mind.

CHAPTER TWELVE

Packing up the next day, I was anxious to get back to Cincinnati and preoccupied with the thought of Detective Mike making any headway with the case. Putting my suitcase in my car, Maribeth and Chad wished me a safe trip.

Chad said, "Hey, take it easy out there," and Melinda said, "Don't forget to stop and eat something along the way," which made me a chuckle a little.

I said that I'd do that, but food was not on the top of my priority list and as I drove down I-29 South to the I-64 West exit, I contemplated all of the suspects that Mike would encounter in his investigation. I was relieved that someone else would be on my side and at least being able to add to the scanty news reports.

I could feel my old Mercedes Benz strain as I headed up the steady incline of the mountains. In front of me there were cars back to back because of the drizzle that had slowed traffic and eighteen wheelers were darting to the fast lane to avoid the slowdown. A supernatural mist permeated around the trees giving them a ghost-like quality and the faint headlights signaled danger. The shamrock green shone onto the trees in shadows that reflected back in streaks of light. Coming up on a car too fast, I hit the brakes and slid barely missing the car in front of me by inches. Screeeech! My body flew forward snapping my neck against the seat. I adjusted my neck back against the seat, stepped on the gas, and headed on down the road. I finally got passed the traffic merged onto the highway headed towards White Sulphur Springs, West Virginia. After getting to Charleston, West Virginia, the rest of the trip went fast except for the minor delay on I-275 and I-71 back to the area of Fairfield, Ohio and, boy, was I glad to get home. I made good time and was home before knew it.

I turned into the large gated community where my neighbors were out and about. Pulling into my reserved parking space, I got my bags out of the car and took them inside. I looked up toward the sky and thanked God to be home. Waving to neighbors and taking my suitcase inside, I hoped that this was the beginning of the end of this ordeal.

****

I got up the next morning with increased energy and vitality. I emailed Mike who emailed back to meet him at his office around 11 am. I wrote up the facts, printed it out, and read it over for anything I left out. The facts were that a young Saudi Arabian student had been conspiring with Loretta to get himself into the university by paying for grades, threatening, and harassing. My report outlined how Loretta had instigated the grade changes, and the University of Cincinnati had been turning a blind eye to the whole scandal. The only question that hadn't been answered was why Loretta was going along with such a sordid cover up. Money from kickbacks was the motive, and when Loretta stopped going along with the plan to admit deficient students, she was murdered. Murdered to avenge the deportations of Saudi students. She never thought that she'd get caught. Dealings were going on with people from other countries – and their cultural view is that it was OK to lie and cheat – if you think that you can get away with it – that's what the Saudi students had told me. Foreign exchange students were influencing and worming their way into the system here, immorally and illegally, through dishonest dealings.

Going down Ronald Reagan Highway east, I took the Collins exit south to Branson Rd. Turning left off of the main road, the homes and businesses gradually became closer and closer together. All of the houses looked basically the same. Small, brick houses with small windows, and they descended in size as the neighborhood got poorer and poorer. The area was run down and the gas station with its cracking and peeling paint had two trucks that looked as if they had been waiting for weeks to be serviced. Three old cars with multiple dents and rusty paint sat over to the side. This was definitely a rough area, and I checked my doors to make sure they were locked. In a small, run-down brick building, I saw the sign, Singleton Detective Agency, and pulled into the side parking lot. Several teenage boys with greasy black hair and tank tops walked down the sidewalk, and I allowed them to get further away before exiting my car. Going up to the door, I was uneasy about the prospect of hiring an investigator but I was compelled to do it. I pulled on the glass door which was locked and then rang the bell. No one showed up so I rang again, looking over my shoulder, my imagination wondering what would happen if a person charged out from behind some bushes – an irrational thought, but possible...

After an endless several minutes, a middle-aged, gaunt woman in thin, worn-out pants and an oversized shirt slowly opened the door and said, "Do you have an appointment with Mike?" Her hunched over posture made her bones protrude from her arms.

"Yes, but I'm a little early."

"Ma'am, he just called and said that he would be here in about five minutes. He had car trouble. I can't let you in because it's official business here."

"Oh, I see, I can wait here," and no sooner than I said that she slammed the wide metal door that I'd questioned if I'd made the right decision in coming here. What I imagined about TV detectives and their glamorous lifestyle of driving expensive cars and wearing designer clothes wasn't proving to be true. While waiting for Mike, I surveyed the area. I saw men doing construction on the rooftop of the building across the street. They were struggling to repair the roof on an old gun shop store and they were holding onto the shingles that were slick and causing them to slide partway down the side. It was scary to watch, and I could tell that they were frustrated by their yelling to warn each other even though I couldn't actually hear their words.

Suddenly, I heard a "Have you been waiting long?" and saw an attractive man emerge from around the corner of the building.

Mike Singleton was all of six feet tall with sandy brown hair and a wide grin. He was wearing baggy pants and a cotton, plaid shirt with leather, western boots. He looked like any average, ordinary guy with not-so-coordinated clothes.

"Hi, I'm Maddie Hauck, and I haven't been waiting long." Searching through a large ring of keys, he said, "Here let me show you in," curiously not asking for any ID or anything. He opened the door and led me down a dingy, dark hallway with several flickering, fluorescent lights and emerald green tiles that looked faded and colorless from wear and tear. That shade of emerald green and reminded me of those almond and lime green refrigerators of the 1970s. This building was creepy; and not a place that anyone would want to meet a total stranger. He turned to the right and put his key into a thin mahogany door that only had a single lock, which jingled on its loose screws. Some security, I thought. The small room looked more like an oversized, walk-in closet rather than a room.

The walls were a raw umber and the floor was so covered with boxes and filing cabinets that there was barely enough space to maneuver around it. There was his mahogany desk in the corner with a client chair off to the side. The wood paneled walls had some scratches and there were square non-opaque glass windows near the top of the walls that yielded a small dim light out of the room. With only a peep hole window allowing in some outside light, the room resembled a cell or dungeon. There were papers scattered everywhere, and I wondered how anyone worked in this disheveled area.

Mike mumbled, embarrassed, "Sorry my office is a little messy." He walked around a brown filing box with loose papers on top. As he sat down and scooted up to his desk, there was so much clutter on the desk that there was only about three inches of space to work. Only the computer and telephone were not covered in the disarrayed office. I sat down and gave him the fact papers and he skimmed them wetting his fingers on a moist sponge and flipping papers so rapidly that it made a snapping noise.

As if talking to himself, Mike said, "Oh I see," and "No leads – not surprising. That could be problematic if there isn't anything to go on."

After some exasperated sighs, I said, "Well, couldn't you just give it a shot and see what you can find?"

On the walls surrounding Mike's desk were many diplomas, including a private investigation certificate and an award for community service and valor. If keeping an organized office wasn't his fortė, then maybe it was because he was so absorbed in work that he had no time to get himself together – at least he acted professionally.

After a few minutes, he said, "Yeah, I can take this case," and I wrote a deposit check and signed the contract papers while he explained some legal phrases on several pages.

Mike said, "Great. First things first. I'll get in touch with the Cincinnati Police or FBI and get the scoop on what they have managed to accomplish so far. It's the end of the year so with officers off for vacation, it might tend to slow things down. I'll give them a call this afternoon."

With an air of relief, I said, "That's it –that's all you need to take on this case? When do you think you'll know something, some facts, some . . . ?"

He said, "Every case is different. Some cases I can wrap up soon but this may take some real investigating to find out if they'll let me in on how it's progressing. I have your number and I'll give you a call if I need anything else."

I mouthed only a faint "thank you" through my lips.

Mike said, "Oh, by the way, since you were threatened, I have to ask, do you carry a weapon to protect yourself?"

"I have pepper spray cannisters and two taser guns – one needs a new battery."

Mike said, "If you bring it in here, I can change the battery for you. I have some extra batteries back in our supply closet."

"Thanks. I'll bring it in sometime."

For some odd reason, that seemed like an abrupt ending to what I expected be some at-length discussion and he stood up signaling that the appointment was over. I thanked him and accepted that I had to wait and wait for someone else to take the lead ...and have patience. And patience was not my virtue.

CHAPTER THIRTEEN

New Year's Eve – New Year's celebrations in Cincinnati had always been the bomb. Despite the bitter cold, I met my friend Gina at the Cincinnati Zoo to watch the fireworks. Gina was a dear friend and a mentor for me when I first started teaching in Cincinnati. She taught me everything about education and I felt indebted to her. Like others in this area, Gina was German, and sometimes made a pronunciation error when she said, "I cannot *recreate* Christmas here like it is in Heidelberg." She meant to *re-create.* Her striking, shoulder-length hair was accented with straight bangs, making her overall features appear harsh against her porcelain white skin. She was always upfront and honest, which I appreciated. Gina had lived in Cincinnati close to the zoo so she could walk there anytime. Since we had always liked the Cincinnati Zoo and been going there for several years, it was practically a tradition to see the fireworks together. Traveling down Clifton Ave, I took several turns and parked near Vine Street. I got out and saw her by the entrance. Families and couples holding hands were wandering around, and I had this eerie feeling that someone was about to mug me, and I pulled my bag closer to me apprehensive of my surroundings. It was bitter cold and my wool gloves itched but it was too painful to take them off.

Smiling, I already saw her but she was excitedly waving to me. Walking up to me she said, "Hey girl, what have been up to lately?"

I said, "Not much, just same ol' problems with the right teaching job."

She said, "If you're still looking for the perfect job, let me tell you, it doesn't exist." That remark slightly offended me.

"Who said that I was searching for the perfect job?" Changing the subject, I said, "How's work at The Enquirer?"

Gina said, "I'm moving up to Assistant Editor when my supervisor retires and that should be around the corner."

"Oh, I'm so excited for you. We'll have to celebrate."

"Thanks but that hasn't happened yet."

"I bet it does. You've worked so hard to get where you are. We should go to Gutenfelder's sometime – my treat."

Gina said excitedly, "Let's do it. It'll inspire me to keep workin' hard."

Gutenfelder's is an excellent German bar and restaurant where people in the city and campus went for drinks. University students, locals, and businessmen enjoyed the German brew and conversed about stats and happenings with the Bengals and Reds.

Strolling around the zoo was a blast but I kept checking my cell phone in some silly notion that I would get some kind of update on whether or not Mike had spoken to the FBI or "gotten on it." It was becoming a compulsive habit. Gina noticed it, and she looked annoyed. "Are you expecting a call from a guy – you can't seem to give your cell a rest."

"It's about the campus murder." "No one is calling you this evening so forget it," and she suddenly saw she was dampening my spirit.

Realizing her slight scolding, she lowered her head in conciliatory repose.

"Whatever you're struggling with, it would be best for you to be proactive about what you can do in your situation."

Gina was an intellectual and I was the opposite – someone in tune with emotions, but this problem was bringing me into a new awareness. I now saw everything in terms of the pain that I was feeling and all events and people were being colored by my pain. Letting go of it was *not* an option for me.

Mike was the person to solve this case. I needed to let go and give him the space to do it *his* way – whatever that was.

****

January was a long month with short days of sun and below zero temperatures that paralyzed the city with forceful winds. In the bitter cold, there was so much energy expended in just getting from place to place. The mid-winter blahs echoed in drab clothing and people scurried with chilled expressions inside buildings to warm up. Despondency could be read in the pale and pallid facial expressions.

In his disheveled office, Mike was searching through piles and pulling out slips of paper with information and cards with contact information. Enormous stacks of papers were strewn on file folders. Mike had brought many criminals to justice and was highly respected despite some of his unconventional methods in tracking down society's worst. But he was one of the best, if not the best in Ohio. Gulping down a ham sandwich and coffee, he brought out the fact sheet that I gave him, reviewed it, and dialed the FBI. He wiped mustard from the corner of his mouth and took a gulp of coffee. He did a quick, cute wink at me, as if showing that he was in charge, and this was a piece of cake for him.

Mike said, "What we need to do is get in touch with Agent Garrett. He's an old friend from our training days at Quantico in Virginia back in the 1990s. He's a good guy. Let's see what he says so we can get this case moving." Dialing the number, he said, "I'll put it on speaker phone."

Maybe if there were some comradeship in the detective world, then we could at least get a handle on what the evidence there was. Tense, I bit down on my lower lip.

An operator in the Crimes Unit answered. "Hello, this is Investigator Singleton and I would like to speak to the agents in charge of the Bryson murder."

The operator sounding taken aback said, "Excuse me, you'd like to speak to who?"

"Yes, this is Investigator Singleton and I would like to speak to Agent Garrett." Special assistants were extra careful in screening calls. "Sir, I'll have to take your name and number."

"My name is Mike Singleton, and I have been hired privately to look into the Bryson murder. My number is 513-999-5132."

"I have it. Agent Garrett will be in touch."

"Thank you ma'am, have a good day."

Several days went by and Mike received no return call despite faxes and phone calls to Agent Garrett and the head of the FBI. One afternoon in mid-January, I decided to give Mike a call. Mike answered coughing and so hoarse I didn't recognize him. "Hello, this is Singleton Investigations. May I help you?"

"Hi, this is Maddie Hauck, and I'm calling about the Bryson case. Have you been able to make any headway?"

Mike was sounding totally out of it. "Oh, Maddie," "Yes, this is Maddie," I interrupted. "I have not been able to speak with one of my colleagues over there at the Bureau. No word back yet. I've been so sick with this bronchitis."

"No word yet," I said, "what's the hold up?" "Who knows? Probably an assistant who only gives him the *classified* messages. Anyway, if I don't hear anything in a day or two, I'll pay a visit and see if that gets the ball rollin.'"

Torn between being disappointed and sympathetic to his illness, I said, "Can you see if they'll talk to you soon?"

"Maddie, you're not my only case."

"I know but this is important to me," he said indignant and defeated.

"And a lot of other people have *important* cases, too."

"Yeah, I was hoping . . ."

"Don't worry, if this case has gotten cold, they'll be beggin' for help."

Our exchange was unpleasant but every day was endless waiting for some answers. Strained. Frustrated. That's how I felt, so I held onto the fact that Mike had a reputation for his successes. Mike never had a doubt that he would be defeated, ever.

CHAPTER FOURTEEN

Meditation, an ancient way of relieving stress, is how I prefer to alleviate my anxiety. When I meditate, I clear my mind and think of all the right things in my life—rather than the wrong things – and there are plenty of people who are suffering much worse than I am. In a peaceful state and listening to water flowing, I am totally relaxed. And it feels so refreshing that I want to meditate and look forward to it, no matter what has been going on that day. I am jolted by the sound of my cell phone on the night stand next to my bed.

"Maddie Hauck?"

"Yes. Who's this?"

I hear an authoritative, "This is Agent Garrett," and I do a double-take now that I'm totally awake. I know that voice.

He says, "I don't know if you've heard about the fire on campus, but Agent Nelson want to ask you some questions about it."

"Um, the fire, I heard about it, but what's that got to do . . ."

"Well, we'd appreciate it if you could come down here."

"I guess I can come down tomorrow. What time?"

"About 10 am would be good." "OK. I'll be down."

In hanging up, and before I knew what I was saying, I realized that I had committed to answering more questions for the FBI, I had to get Mike on the phone.

I was slightly apprehensive about asking him to go with me.

"Hello. Singleton Detective Agency. How may I help you?"

"Uh, this is Maddie Hauck." "Maddie, what's up now?" as if he's forgotten about our previous exchange.

"Well, Agent Garrett called me and they want me to come down to FBI headquarters to answer some questions about the campus fire. I *don't* know anything about the fire."

Unconcerned, Mike said, "So what's the problem? You go down there and answer their questions and then get the heck outta there."

"Yeah, if I don't know anything, then how long could it last?"

"I could drive you down there and ask him some questions in person. Kinda spur of the moment and who knows? If he even has the time, but ..."

Almost begging, I said, "Could you *please* do that for me?"

"Yeah, no problem."

"Are you feelin' better?"

"Yeah, I'm doin' much better, thanks." "What time does he want to meet with you?"

"10 a.m."

"OK. I'll be at your place at 9 am sharp. Sounds like a plan. See ya in the mornin'."

With that I said, "Yeah, have a nice evenin'" and hung up. In some strange way, this might be working out for me.

Waking up the next morning, I felt utter dread. Dread at having to make the trip down and dread of being asked a bunch of questions. I didn't want to face the agent again under any circumstances. I slipped on my nice blouse and dark gray pinstriped blazer and pants. My flat, black leather shoes with a Puritan-like buckle pinched my toes but I didn't want to wear high-heels because I had to walk down city streets to get to the FBI headquarters. Unlike most days when I procrastinated to leave home, I was ready at 8:50 am and sat down to think about what questions I might be asked and wonder if Mike would be here on time. At 9 am, I looked out to see a Ford Escort tearing down the drive and pulling up to my front door. A Ford Escort? Didn't detectives drive cooler cars? But I was relieved that he was here. I got my purse, locked up, and as I was walking down the sidewalk, I see him open the door for me with a smile.

"Mornin, how are ya?"

"I'm fine and ready to get this over with."

"Oh. I hear ya. This has gotta be hard on you."

"Yeah, it's hard on me. And not being able to work full time with the added expense of this case."

"Oh, I know that this will be finished before the year's out."

I thought, before the year is out? We're just beginning a new year. Mike didn't say anything. He changed the subject by saying, "It'll be a real surprise if I can get in to see Agent Garrett, and we should get a leg up on how the case is going."

Guess I was putting too much pressure on him and he sensed it. We got on I-71 and headed downtown. We took the McCormick Exit and merged onto Edison Drive down the street from FBI headquarters. Mike paralleled parked into a space on the street. He said, "This is close enough to the building." We got out onto a wide sidewalk where people in business suits who were carrying attache cases were making their way down the sidewalk, with heads that looked over the top of the person in front of them. Walking up to the building, Mike somehow looked slightly out of place compared to the other men who were wearing nice suits. He was wearing an aviator's jacket and moccasin-type shoes – a little casual for a meeting. Taking the elevator to the seventh floor, the door opened and a secretary, behind a desk, wearing a pin-stripe blazer with a wool cardigan sweater and cat glasses, was speaking on the phone but noticed Mike and me directly in front of her.

Looking above her glasses, she said to the person on the phone, "Well, gotta go."

She said curtly to me, "Ma'am, do you have an appointment with someone here?"

I responded, "I have an appointment with Agent Garrett."

Mike piped in, "And I am a detective with Singleton Detective Agency, here to support Ms. Hauck."

"Oh, I see," as if she were unaccustomed to in-person clients. "Let me see if Agent Garrett can see you."

She got on her phone and told him that we were here, and then told us to go down the hall for the last office on the right. The open office had windows all around overlooking downtown and there were cubicles and a large map and international clocks on the wall, showing the time in various cities–London, Beijing, Paris, and Moscow. The offices on the interior had many cubicles and most workers were talking on the phone and jotting down information, while the outer offices were fewer and had a clear view of the downtown vicinity. I stopped at the door and at that moment, Agent Garrett appeared at the entrance to his door. He looked at me and then at Mike.

With noticeable surprise, Agent Garrett said, "Well, well, if it isn't my ol' buddy Mike Singleton. What brings you to the FBI?" They shook hands like they were two old classmates at a high school reunion.

"How've ya been? I'm still working at my agency but I've been hired by Ms.

Hauck here to help out on a case."

Agent Garrett said, "Let me show you into my office where we can talk about this in private."

We went into a small office that had three file cabinets and some neatly stacked files and recording equipment on a small, table. This office felt sterile compared to Mike's office.

Curious, he said, "So let me get this straight, Mike. You're here to assist Ms. Hauck as she answers some questions for us."

Mike said, "Yes. I am here to make sure that she is supported with whatever she needs."

Agent Garrett said, "They're really routine questions, but we have to be as thorough as possible with an arson investigation."

The tone had changed to official business as they proceeded. "Let me first ask Ms. Hauck a few questions so I can get that out of the way."

Turning to me, he said, "Ms. Hauck, I just need to get my file here." He opened a manilla file folder and looked through some notes. "This is about the arson on the UC campus that happened recently." I knew why I was here so I figured he was thinking out loud.

"Yes, that's right."

"Do you know or have any knowledge of who started the fire?"

I said, "No, I don't know who did it."

"Did you hear anyone on campus talk about *any* fires that were being set on campus?" I looked over at Mike and answered, "I heard a couple of colleagues talk about some students who were setting fires to some of the buildings."

"Oh, I see. Who were your colleagues that were talking about the arson? I've gotta have their names and information about how to get in contact them."

I put my hand on my head. "Um, one instructor was Derek Jenney and the other colleague was Jim Pauley.

"And what were the students' names? Do you recall any first or last names?"

"No, sir, I don't."

Looking at both Mike and me, Agent Garrett said, "Arson cases are tough when the evidence doesn't provide any suspects. But I'll see what I can get outta these two." I was taken aback that he was talking as much about this case, but Mike was there and that might have made a difference. All I knew was that I felt more comfortable with him at my side. Agent Garrett wrote down my former colleagues' phone numbers, and he closed the file with a sigh.

Mike said, "Now, about the Bryson case. What have you been able to find out so far?"

Agent Garrett said, "We've been trying to get our lists of people to interview, but it's been slow going with the university. UC claims that they want to cooperate, but they have been draggin' their feet."

Mike inquired intently, "What evidence do you have at this point that could narrow that list down?"

Agent Garrett shrugged. "Without much evidence at the scene, we don't have anything to go on... but we have to interview anyone who had access to the building. We're in the process of setting up those interviews."

Mike asked, "And could I be with you and Agent Nelson for those interviews?"

A slight pause. "Uh, first, I'll need to check in with Agent Nelson and Chief Agent Simons about that. He's the head honcho here. Everything goes through him for approval."

Persuasively, Mike said, "Hey, you know my reputation for solving cases."

"Oh, yeah, I know, but we just have to be sure of your credentials and for him to sign off on it."

"Yes, we've gotta have that."

Agent Garrett said, "I'll do my best because I have this strange feeling that it's going to turn out to be a real stinker of a case to solve."

Mike said, "Here's my card and let me know when the interviews start."

"Sure thing, buddy." Agent Garrett said to me, "Thanks for coming in today," and I only tilted my head in compliance. They shook hands and it was a rather awkward moment as the visit had been a mix of business and personal issues and Mike wondered to himself if he hadn't come off like an amateur ball player begging to play in the big leagues.

Mike drove me home and escorted me up to my door. "Give ya a call when I know something more."

"Thanks. I've gotta work tomorrow. At least that'll keep me busy."

CHAPTER FIFTEEN

In the dead of winter, the weight of work hangs heavy and dark days are endless in anticipation of spring. Iced over lakes take days and weeks to melt and waiting for the warmth of spring brings joy to the new season.

Getting home from school and watching the gray sky fall on granite hills, I wanted to sleep and hibernate from the mental fatigue. Around 5 p.m. with dimming skies, my cell phone began to ring with Mike's name showing up as one of my contacts I added him since I knew that we would be working on this for the long haul.

I said, "What's up Mike?"

"I was just calling to let you know that Agent Nelson and I have set up the interviews to be done down at Geisler Hall. They have weeded out some suspects but they are still so many, and bringing them all into headquarters could be a major problem. There's just so many of them."

"Oh," is all I muttered.

"Chief Simons and Agent Nelson have approved it for me to conduct interviews with them."

"Oh that's good news."

"Yeah I guess. To be honest, we don't know if we can ever pin down who committed this crime from the evidence, but we're gonna do our best to talk to as many people possible."

"Well, at least it's a start."

"Do you wanna tag along and stay on campus or do you wanna me to call you during our breaks?"

"I wanna know something soon. Can I meet you somewhere on campus for updates? I could check out the library for books and resources."

"Yeah, that'd be better than discussing it on the phone. But I have to warn you, it's gonna be a *long* day."

****

Walking out of the Carlson Parking Garage, I walked down the steep embankment, passed the gym and police and security offices to Geisler Hall. I saw Mike some distance away and his hair was blowing in the wind, and his hands were buried inside his pockets. Shivering, he looked cold, pale, and sallow.

Without any hello, he said, "Looks like they're setting up inside." He leaned over and could see down into a room below ground level. Inside, Agent Garrett and Agent Nelson were inside arranging chairs and setting up the recording equipment. They were moving the desks and chairs so that Mike would be one side and the suspect they were questioning would be on the other side. I could see Agent Nelson testing a microphone to see if it was working.

Mike said, "I guess it's time to for me to get in there and help."

Anxious to get in the last word, I responded, "When you take a break, give me a call. I'll be here or over at the library."

Mike was already half inside the door by the time I finished my sentence. He went through another set of doors, and I could see that he was talking to the agents.

The Agents sat down first behind the desk and Mike took a seat at the smaller, metal chair off to the side. Agent Garrett pulled his briefcase up onto the desk and removed the list of suspects, marking off names and writing quickly. Through the window, I saw Agent Nelson look directly up at me. It was obvious to me that he was asking Mike about why I was there. Mike looked up at me without wanting to explain why I was there. I knew what was going to happen – Mike was going to tell Agent Nelson that I was hanging onto this case like a leech, and that I wasn't letting go until it was solved. Agent Nelson had a peculiar smile, and I didn't know if it was he was perturbed that I was observing or amused that a client had accompanied their detective on a case. Agent Nelson proceeded through the doors towards me. I didn't know if he was about to let me have it for acting like an overseer or foreperson in their investigation.

Instead, Agent Nelson walked over to me with a sheepish look and said, "So I see that you're totally invested in this case. We're trained in how to solve these crimes. This is not our first rodeo."

I argued, "I want this case solved so I can get my life back. And the students on campus can stop being put on edge. They're even in fear during the day walking to class. It's scary for them."

Agent Nelson touched my arm very delicately. "I don't know what Mike is telling you, but we *do* have leads, and we're working on this as much as we can with all of our other cases."

Complaining, I said, "I know, I know … Mike has already told me that I'm not your only case."

Agent Nelson said, "If you want, we can have lunch, and I can share some tidbits of info with you."

I could tell that he was embarrassed and it was almost too personal to look him in the eyes because he was timid. That didn't fit what I thought an FBI agent would be. . . .

I smiled and said, "OK. I'll meet you here when you have a break."

He said, "One o'clock. Meet me here and we'll walk somewhere. Traffic is such a bear at this time of day."

And I confirmed, "One o'clock it is."

And he gave me a flirtatious smile. I felt like a young school girl on a first date. Directing my attention back to the campus, I saw students lugging backpacks, occasionally stopping to buy a newspaper or gravitating towards the places where they could buy a doughnut or sweet roll. With the penetrating cold passing through my bones, I walked toward the library and up the steps to the revolving door. Pushing through and walking around, I stopped to look up at the spacious room and rows of computers.

Seated in front of me was a librarian who looked European with platinum blonde hair, and she looked above as I approached her desk. I asked, "Where are the newspapers?"

She said with a French accent, "Zey are back on zee wall."

I said, "Oh, I see them back there."

"Just let me know if zer iz any zing else that you need."

"Thank you."

Strolling past the computers, I saw students in oversized sweatshirts and torn jeans laboring away on computers, intent on course assignments. Reaching the aisle with the newspapers, I picked up the USA Today and found a very comfy leather chair near a window. From a long, rectangular window that stretched from the ceiling to the floor, the sun shone down on me in rays of warmth. Stories of worldwide violence plagued each page. Only one positive article was to be found and it was about a man who had saved an older gentleman from a burning car. That was it. Peering out the window to the courtyard below, I spotted two teenagers walking hand in hand and stopping at a bench to chat and kiss. They were such an attractive couple and their intimacy was adorable. I felt like dozing off in the warmth of the sun, but took out my phone to wait for a call from Mike. Da-ding, da-ding... the rings from my phone resonated even louder in this quiet library.

I said, "Hey Mike, what's up?"

"Sounds like I woke you."

"No, I'm just resting my eyes."

"Did you find out anything?"

"Let's meet at Starbuck's and we'll talk."

"Gotcha. Be there in five minutes."

Groggy, I got up and headed up the hill. I stood under the canopy while drips of water hit my head making me duck and move closer to the door. A long line of students texting on cell phones stood in front of me.

Out of nowhere, Mike tapped me on the shoulder.. "What would you like?"

I said, "Frappuccino. And what would you like?"

"Something with mega caffeine. A double espresso." He opened his wallet searching for money.

"I've got it. Don't worry about it." I paid for both of us.

"That is nice. Thanks."

We got our drinks, climbed the steps and sat down at a round table. The music was blaring loud and Mike asked the barista if could turn it down a little. The music was attenuated by our moving to another table behind an oriental-style divider in the middle of the room.

The barista asked politely, "Is that better?"

Mike said, "Yeah, thanks much."

So all we heard were students laughing and talking in the background. I tapped the side of my cup and it was too hot to touch.

"Ouch! Watch out, that's hot!" So I decided to broach the subject of what went on in during the interviews. Mike took out a large stack of papers clipped together with folders in the middle.

He said, "There's quite a bit to sort through. There's forensics, examiner's report, pictures of evidence. . ." as he laid the stacks of papers in several piles. I was expecting a more direct response about who they interviewed.

Glancing at one page, Mike said, "There are pages of people to interview. And I mean that literally, pages."

"Ugh. No surprise. Who did you interview today?"

"We interviewed two people. Kathleen Vegera and a Derek Edelson."

"Huh, that's it?" revealing my displeasure.

"Maddie, we had to question them, take note, and review it. It takes time and it's gonna take even more to question all of these people," as his eyes scanned down the list of names.

"So what did you get out of Kathy and Derek?"

Mike was hesitant to say much, probably from fatigue, but I sensed that for some reason, he didn't want to tell me what was transpiring between the agents and himself. But I was paying for him to get information, so I felt entitled to have everything. An inchoate case and little information weren't flying with me. Mike had pictures though. The first was of Kathleen, a young woman with no makeup, freckles, and straight brown hair that she wore in a braid down her back. She looked like she could be a model for an organic foods company with her natural and clean appearance.

He said, "To us, Kathleen appeared to lack the opportunity. She was oblivious and unphased about campus happenings and too focused on her partner and gettin' by moneywise. It was kinda funny how she talked."

"How she talked?"

"Well, whenever she talked, the tone of her voice would go up at the end. It sounded like she was asking *us* questions, even though she was making statements."

"Oh. Women talk like that. Just uncertainty or lack of confidence. Who else did you interview?"

"We interviewed Joshua Edelson."

Mike looked at a picture of Joshua which showed a bald man with a small scar on the side of his face.

"He was, uh, too incapable of pulling something like that off."

"Whaddya mean?"

"He is disgruntled at being the office boy, the grunt, whatever you call him.

He had an acrid relationship with administration and instructors because he felt slighted at not getting a teaching position, so he didn't take to kindly to being stuck in this subservient position. I don't buy that he was in any way connected to the murder. He is too . . ."
Anxious to know about the Saudi student, I said with intensity, "Did you interview Fahad Faruq?"

"Not yet."

"Not yet? He's the prime suspect!"

"He's on the list for when... let me see. Yeah, next week."

"Next week? But he could be on a plane getting the heck outta Dodge by then."

"Maddie, we can't hold people without evidence. You have to let law enforcement do their job. They'll solve it, and I predict that it'll be by the end of summer."

"Yeah, but by the time that they have the real evidence, the suspects will have gone to a country that doesn't extradite."

Conciliatory, Mike said, "I think that there is more than just a murder here to solve. You should consult an attorney about how you were treated as a whistleblower."

I said, "Me? A whistleblower?

"Yeah, you put the spotlight on people who were engaging in unethical acts, and they retaliated against you. Isn't that illegal?"

I was dumbfounded. I said, "I suppose you're right. I did have a hand in exposing what was happening on campus and behind closed doors. Maybe I should consult someone about my rights."

"I think that your civil rights were violated – big time."

"Maybe."

End of summer to me was a long time in the future to get some resolution to this case. Mike's phone starting ringing, and while he took the call, I thought, end of summer? That was eons from now.

After wrapping up his call, he acted as if he had totally forgotten what we were talking about and only said, "Don't worry. We'll get this case movin'."

CHAPTER SIXTEEN

After spending a boring morning walking around and visiting the new shops in the area, I walked across campus to meet Agent Nelson for lunch. I was traversing the campus along the side of the football field when I heard sirens blaring and getting louder and louder. I put my hands over my ears to muffle the piercing sound. The police and ambulance stopped at the west part of campus at the corner of the parking garage. The police and paramedics rushed to two-story side landing with a roof that juts out from the third floor. Several students stand in the entryway to the garage and one student's mouth is quivering. They point above and to the side where the emergency personnel are running up the embankment toward the landing. While the paramedics went into full rescue mode, another female paramedic who looked a little shaken took out a sheet and covered the body. By this time, the police were scrambling to contain the scene and other students had congregated along the sidewalk.

I asked one student, "Who is the deceased?"

And the student responded, "It's a male Chinese student. People are saying that he was wearing athletic clothes so they don't know if he fell … or jumped."

I said, "Oh, that's incredibly sad that a student would jump . . . if that is what happened."

The student said, "It is terrible, but some international students here feel so much stress to get good grades, get into grad school, and make their parents proud. Some students just can't hack the pressure. Too much."

As much as I despised this tragic episode, I was mesmerized watching how they processed the scene and how they transported the deceased body out. Then people continued on their way. And I was left with some lingering doubts that this should be investigated to find out it was related to Loretta's murder.

****

By meeting Agent Nelson I thought that I could actually find out what had been transpiring behind the scenes and talk to someone who was willing to give me details. I went inside the building to the grand lobby to wait but didn't want Mike to see me there. There was no place that I could see Agent Nelson without being spotted by Mike, so I walked down to the corner and stood at the intersection waiting for Agent Nelson to emerge at 1:00. I probably looked very suspicious as I strained my neck over like a crane expectant of Agent Nelson to emerge. At 1:00, Mike walked out and went straight for his car which was parked on the street. After he had taken off, I saw Agent Nelson come out and I started walking toward him. As Agent Garrett came through the doors, I stopped and waited for him to keep walking down the hill. Finally, Agent Nelson was alone. I walked toward him and didn't know what to say. Slightly nervous, slightly optimistic.

Casually, he said, "Ready to get some lunch?"

I said, "Yep, I'm ready."

"OK. Then follow me so we can go somewhere a little more *private.*"

He gave me a half-smile and I felt like I was getting mixed messages. Was this about the case – or something else? I don't know but I was really curious and thought that I'd play along. When the traffic light turned green, we took off across the street very fast. It was difficult to keep up with his fast pace up a hill, bypassing shops, as we traversed away from the campus. On the way, we passed a mom-and-pop drugstore that had a faded sign with an old-time ice cream float on it. Next, we went by a tacky theater that had flashing lights and trash cans with candy and cigarette butts all around it. After turning a corner, the neighborhood changed drastically. There were upscale attorney's offices and older, well-maintained homes that had been renovated. The lawns were immaculate, and the people leaving the offices were dressed in suits and stylish clothes. Agent Nelson gestured toward a small sandwich shop "Lewis Cafe," that had a sign out front with fishing memorabilia. The atmosphere was quiet with only a few businessmen sitting at a table, and the table and chairs were rustic. The lighting was dark with hanging lamps and the side was lit up over the bar.

Agent Nelson said, "This booth will do." And I sat down across from him in the booth with its back that extended well above my head.

Getting the courage to speak, I said, "Tell me about what you and Agent Garrett have been uncovering with the case."

Agent Nelson said, "Maddie, I can call you Maddie?"

"Yes, of course. And I call you Agent Nelson?" And I giggled embarrassingly.

"Oh. Please call me Ian."

"I'll do that," taming my giddiness.

The waitress came over and recommended the fish sandwiches and we both ordered that with coffee. Glancing at the décor of the restaurant, I said, "Do you eat here often?"

"Sometimes, since it is close to downtown and I have to get away *on occasion.*"

"On occasion? I see. When your job is driving you totally crazy."

"Yeah, you've got that right, but any job has its stresses, and the stress of my *ex-wife.*"

I was so startled at his response that I didn't know how to respond. At that awkward moment, he said, "Yeah, it's been a tumultuous time for me – and my son, since she cannot care for even herself because she is emotionally unstable." And he noticeably held back some sadness and straightened up to regain some composure.

Changing the subject back to the case, Ian said authoritatively, "In any investigation, we have to check out the victim, in this case, Loretta Bryson, with job, personal life, finances, and so forth. We have to ascertain whether or not a person, or persons, had the motive based on their relationships – relationships with *everyone.*"

I said, "And that includes people who worked with the victim I suppose? Even people getting a kickback?"

"Uh, I don't know if we or any law enforcement can be that presumptuous. We have to look at *every* aspect of the victim's life."

"And what did Loretta have hiding in her closet?"

"This may surprise you, but we had investigated her long before this case."

My eyes widened and I gazed around the room – no one was paying attention to us but conscious of eavesdroppers, I lowered my voice –sibilant and softly.

Ian continued, "Some years ago, back in 2004, Loretta Bryson had been working as an administrator at an all girl's private school, and over time, there had been some accusations coming forward from parents that Loretta had been stealing money from some accounts at the school. They demanded that she leave and she left in disgrace."

I whispered, "Oh, my God. Then how did she get this position at UC?

Ian shook his head, "We don't know but from the day that we found out that she was murdered, we were suspicious that money was changing hands and someone was not too pleased with how they didn't get what they paid for."

I said, "Whoa. That woman had a past. So you and Agent Garrett think that her money problems were the reason she was murdered?"

Ian said skeptically, "There are other possibilities. There's the possibility that a former instructor that she fired wanted to get back at her."

"Oh, I know, there was an instructor, Nancy Jarvis, who fought back because she argued with administration that she was let go unfairly."

Ian said, "Then again, there's always the chance that this was just a random act of violence by someone who wanted petty cash, then panicked and killed her when she tried to call for help."

Wary, I said, "I dunno. Do you suspect any personal problems?'

"We can't pin down exactly where Loretta's ex-husband was that night, but we are keeping tabs on him."

Taking a long, deep breath, I said, "Multiple theories and lots of suspects. I get now why it's tough to solve any crime."

"Yeah, that's the way it goes in our world."

The waitress showed up with our food and we ate and talked about Cincinnati and trivial things compared to the murder. After we finished, Ian left some money on the table and we left. Sprinkles turned into pouring rain, and we both pulled our raincoats over our heads to keep the rain off, but we were still drenched without an umbrella. We ran towards the awning of the movie theater and watched the rain as it streamed down the gulley and down the hill in a flowing current. The water that splashed from the awning like a miniature rapid waterfall spraying us from head to toe – and it felt wonderful.

In silence, we both watched the rain and stayed huddled together. Before this day, I had always thought of rain as a nuisance but it was curiously romantic – and I liked it. Our clothes were soaked and we only had to laugh. It was exhilarating to be with this agent and I didn't want it to end. He leaned over and kissed me. It was a long, passionate kiss and we stayed there with chaos going on around us. I knew in some strange way that I wanted to be with him and that there was something magnetic about him. I had to admit to myself that I was smitten with him. We had somehow become connected amid these horrible circumstances. We were in another world for those few minutes when the torrential rain battered us with a shower of rain that left us soaked with squishy clothes and squeaky shoes. And my female intuition with its emotional barometer signaled that this was a good man.

When the rain subsided, I said, "I guess it's time for you to get back to the interviews. How're gonna explain how you got so wet?"

Ian said amusingly, "I'll refuse to answer any questions. That's what agents do when they don't want to answer what goes on while they're not on duty."

"I see."

We walked back to campus where we separated and I left to go home and he headed back to the building. I repeated the name "Ian," like a silly little girl with her first boyfriend. As I passed the slummy, squat buildings on the way to my car, I saw a young, handsome man waving at me. It was Raja, a 20-ish student who was from Saudi Arabia. He had been in my class, and I remembered him because of his creative ideas and ambition to study business. Raja had dark hair and his bulging arms and attractive facial features looked like a person out of the movies. His rugged clothing and the smell of cigarettes made him all the more masculine. He looked glad to see me.

"Teacher, what are you doing on campus? Are you teaching here again?

I was dumbfounded about how to answer. "I, I am investigating what happened to Ms. Bryson. You read and hear about it, I guess . . ."

"Yes, it was terrible what happened to her. All of the students from Saudi Arabia were sad for her. They miss her."

His demeanor exuded sincerity, and his words were thoughtful.

I was very afraid to broach the subject of her murder, but I asked him, "What are you hearing from the students about her murder? What are they saying about the killer?

"They're saying that that group was involved in it."

"What group – the students who were into drugs?

Raja shook his head no as if that had been an unbelievable response. "No, no, teacher. They claim that the Japanese students did it."

That seemed truly absurd to me –that the Japanese students had anything to do with the murder. They were wealthy, studied hard, and respected instructors unlike any other students. Feeding me stories about students that I knew had no involvement disturbed me, so getting out of this conversation was in my best interest.

"Japanese students – why do you say that?" playing along with this ridiculous notion.

"Japanese students don't want to work all the time. They want to party, too. And they're afraid of the shame of parents and people at home just as we are."

I understood what he was talking about --"losing face" – but there had never been any indication that Japanese students would get violent. Raja reminded me of every other student who fed a teacher a pack of lies when he knew very well the real story. But I didn't have any more time to engage in this absurd dialogue.

"Yeah, I suppose. I've gotta get back to work." That was my excuse to leave.

"I hope you come back to teach me sometime. I'd like that."

I didn't know if his statements were said to deliberately obfuscate or he was being sincere in what he was saying. Anyway, I was confused by his accusations and didn't know if I should keep this to myself or bother Mike with misleading evidence – another error that would confound the investigation with impertinent information– and that's probably all it was – a wild goose chase.

CHAPTER SEVENTEEN

My next step involved research into whistleblower laws at the downtown law library in Cincinnati. I was having car trouble so taking the bus downtown was my only option. Taking the bus downtown is an experience – an unpleasant one with the hassles – but definitely one in which you encounter some real characters. There were about ten other people waiting at the bus stop, and I was anxious for the bus to hurry up and arrive, which was sensed by another passenger, a man who was standing next to me.

The man had black skin that was as deep as onyx and he was very neatly dressed in linen pants and shirt. He asked me, "What's your hurry? Are you in dire need to get somewhere?" He had an African accent, and his friendliness ingratiated me to take up a conversation with him.

I said, "We've all been waiting for the bus to come for a while." I looked at my watch. "Do you think it's gonna be here soon?"

He said, "It'll be here before you know it. Do you live around here?"

"Yeah, I live over in the townhouses over there." And I pointed to my complex in the distance.

The man continued. "Well, I am a pastor at the church of God. My name is Olufemi. I came here from Senegal to preach the word of God. If you need to find a church, please visit us."

I said, "Oh, thank you. I'm not going to a church now, but in the future if I . . ."

He interrupted, "You should go to church 'cause we need to be obedient in this life."

I didn't know what to say to his invitation. He seemed honest but for some reason I felt skeptical of him. Anyone could introduce themselves and with good motives, but truthfulness and people who were interested in helping anyone, especially strangers, was elusive to me.

After waiting about 25 minutes, I got on the bus at Franklin Street and barely made it onto the first step as the bus doors snapped shut in back of me. After the passengers in front of me paid, I fed coins into the machine like tokens in a slot machine in Vegas. Crowded and stuffy, the air stagnated and whiffs of rosemary perfume and strong colognes permeated the air. I made my way down to the middle of the aisle when the bus driver bolted forward causing everyone standing to grab the overhead hanging handles to balance ourselves and not fall. I swung around to a six-inch vacancy in the interior of the bus and held tightly to the railing in front. The seat was so slick it almost felt oily, and my derriere slid forward and back in unison to the stops and starts the bus driver made with assertiveness. I was shoved close to the metal side and the pressed my face against the window. Olufemi sat close to me protecting me as a mother wolf would her cubs. When two teenagers boarded the bus, Olufemi guarded me against the teenagers who were talking loudly and canvassing the passengers in a sweeping assessment of who might be a good target. He kept the teenagers from getting too close to me, and after passing several streets, the sign light blinked and the teenagers got off. Olufemi kept his arm from other passengers who might cause me harm. When entering the city, he simply said to me,

"Have a blessed day and hope to see you again." And he was gone.

As the bus departed the suburbs and entered the city, the bus almost lulled me to sleep as the back-and-forth rhythm caused my eyes to blink in a drowsy stare in which Ihad to concentrate on where to exit. Several minutes later, Converse Street came up on the names of streets at the front, and I exited near the library. Down the street and up the steep steps, I noticed the cameras taping visitors in the lobby. The spacious library housed books on every topic, and the books that resided in the Reserve room were kept neatly on shelves in pristine condition. An older, bald man with a sallow complexion, agate eyes, and several strands of hair that he combed to cover his shiny head was shelving books. He moved slowly, and his high, baggy pants held up with plaid suspenders and whistling, and is grandfatherly voice reminded me of Jimmy Stewart in old movies. A library assistant approached him, and he directed the employee to another section. This librarian embodied the expertise of research methods.

I sauntered over toward him and shyly whispered, "Excuse me, do you know where I can find information on legal cases, cases about workplace rights?"

He cupped his hand around his ear to indicate that he couldn't hear well. "Ma'am, did you say that you were looking for cases on workplace rights?"

"Yes, I'm looking for any books, well legal cases, on employer-employee relations, specifically on recent whistleblower cases?"

He scratched his head and pulled his glasses above his head. "Let me see. Those kinds of books are actually on the shelves in the reserve room, and that's in the main area. I'll show you."

He showed me the reserve room with books covering the walls and more books in pristine bookcases in the middle. He stopped abruptly and leaned over squinting his eyes to see the fine print on some book spines.

He mumbled to himself, "Here we are. Books on all types of cases. Personal injury, criminal and civil cases . . . Everything that we have is right here, ma'am."

I said, "Thanks," and he left and went back to shelving books. I found numerous cases on employer-employee relations and whistleblower cases. The whistleblower cases were all on federal court cases against the government, but I copied some cases to my flash drive and spent the evening reading the cases. Now I could appreciate how tedious it is to find out the truth and legal means by which someone has to prove a case.

CHAPTER EIGHTEEN

Today was the day that I decided to find out if I had any case as a whistleblower against the University – or any case for that matter. Employment attorneys were a dime a dozen, but finding one that actually took your case was another. And it all boiled down to money. If they don't determine that you can force the hand of the person who wronged you, then you couldn't claim much damage – and damages to an attorney mean bucks, big bucks. Nevertheless, I located an employment attorney in Hamilton, Ohio by the name of Charles Blankenship. His website was impressive with how he had gone up against the largest companies in order to get compensation for his clients. That's what I wanted, an agressive attorney who would represent me with the relentlessness of a viper that refused to let go. I made an appointment with Mr. Blankenship's secretary and headed off for the city of Hamilton. Taking the curvy roads north up Dixie Highway and into the city on I-27 north, I got closer to the building along a side street called Fenwick Avenue. Some of the houses were boarded up and the other buildings had dilapidated fences that anyone could jump over and be almost on the front step. Pulling into the drive to the office, I parked under a shaded tree and noticed a sign that read, Entrance in back. Heading around the corner of the office, I stopped dead in my tracks. There was a dark-skinned man with curly hair underneath a cap and a t-shirt that had the words devil and Satan painted in swirly writing all over it. He looked me in the eyes and slowly pulled out a switchblade that he held low and close to his thigh. In a sinister voice, with his mouth moving in gyrations, he said, "Hand it over. Give me your purse." I was stunned. I carefully reached into my purse and tossed my wallet to him." He caught it in an overhand movement and jumped the rickety fence in the yard next door. Being closer to my car than the office, I ran to my car and got in jamming my toe against my shoe. Fumbling with my phone, I dialed 9-1-1.

"9-1-1. What's your emergency?"

"I've just been robbed by a man who stole my wallet."

"What's your name, location, and a description of the person?"

I battled to get control of my words. "I, I'm on Progress Avenue in Hamilton."

"What's the address?"

"I'm at 2245 Progress Avenue at the office of Charles Blankenship."

"Can you describe the suspect?"

"He is short, with a cap, and a t-shirt that has devil written all over it."

"Which way did he go?"

"He jumped the fence and took off... I don't know which way he ran."

"We'll send someone out there. Just wait there. Can you think of any other information?"

I got the feeling that I should have been able to describe him better but it all happened so fast. I was about to be knifed.

I said, "No, that's it," and looking down I felt something wet on my toe. It was bleeding from the pumps that had dug into my toe when I ran back to my car. I was covered in perspiration. Several minutes later, I heard the police car turn into the driveway. I got out of my car and walked over to the squad car with two police officers who didn't even get out of their car.

"Are you the person who was held up?"

I said, "Yeah, and he took off over that fence," pointing to the fence that was about to collapse from the boards that had been loosened by the suspect jumping over it.

The officer said, "Give us the information and we'll see if we can track him down and recover your wallet." And when he saw the blood running out from my toe, he asked, "Do you need an ambulance or medical assistance?"

I said, "No, I think it's OK," and I sat down on the knee-high wall around a stone fountain that spouted water. Wiping away the blood, I felt that I had escaped what could have been the end of my life. But I survived. The next half hour I gave the officers my information and that was it. They told me to call someone to drive me home, but that wasn't possible. It was 10:45 am and my appointment was supposed to have been at 9:45. I was an hour late but went into the office to see if I could salvage anything from the rest of this day.

Inside the attorney's office, there was a desk with a lady who checked my ID and asked me my appointment time with Mr. Blankenship. I said, "I'm so sorry I missed my appointment at 9:45, but a man just stole my wallet."

The secretary, astonished, said, "Oh my word. Here in this area?"

I said, "Right out there in the parking lot. I'm late because I was giving the police information about what happened."

She said, "Oh, my goodness. If that had happened to me, I wouldn't have been able to even make my appointment. Let me talk to Mr. Blankenship and see if he can work you in."

She called Mr. Blankenship's office on the intercom system. I could hear her telling him my predicament, and she was able to convince him to see me, albeit an hour late. She strained her neck in order to speak over the desk wall, and said, "Just sit tight. He'll see you shortly. Can I bring you anything to drink? A cup of coffee?"

I said, "Thank you so much, but I'm fine."

About a half hour later, the secretary called my name and led me through some glass French doors to a spacious office that was exquisitely decorated with a large desk and shelves of decorations, and a silver vase filled with beautiful magnolias and jonquils that gave the room a sweet aroma over the cottony paper smell of the law books. On the walls were large framed diplomas of Mr. Blankenship's college and kaw school degrees, and other honors. I couldn't help but notice a ceramic pot with a large top that had a note painted on it. The message said, Ashes of former clients. Hmm, that's amusing, I thought. There were also pictures of Mr. Blankenship and his children at the beach and horseback riding. What a life. Several minutes later, Mr. Blankenship entered the room from the side door. He was short and his oversized suit made him look childish. He had curly red hair and his pasty white complexion made him appear anemic. He reached across his desk to shake my hand.

"How are you today, Ms. Hauck?" He was soft spoken.

"I'm fine now except for the incident in the parking lot."

"Yes, my secretary told me. Are you all right?"

"I'm fine. I just needed to get some counsel on a *possible* case against the University of Cincinnati."

"What advice do you need?" He cleared his throat.

"I was wondering if I had a case against the University for the retaliation in bringing the cheating scandal to light. They forced me out and I feared for my life."

Mr. Blankenship rubbed his chin in contemplation. "Uh, let me see. Did they retaliate on any grounds that violated you such as with age, race, disability, or sexual orientation?"

"No, it doesn't have to do with that. It has to do with retaliation according to whistleblower laws."

"Do you have any written documentation that states that they are taking action against you based on your exposure of them in their misconduct?" His inquiry pinpointed the heart of my problem – no written documentation – and that is so unfair.

"No, but it happened." I recognized the problem with this case.

"It would be a hard case to win even if they did retaliate against you for being a whistle blower. Employers have to show that they violated your civil rights, and even then it takes so much time and money to bring a case." He was doubtful in his response.

"How much does it cost?" I asked.

"It's about $40,000, and that's why employees go their way – and why employers get away with bullying and injustices. Maybe someday this country will have stricter laws like Europe or Australia. Their employers have to take action and protect employees."

Embarrassed, I asked, "What do I owe you today?"

He said, "Thirty dollars, and my secretary will handle it."

I shook hands and thanked him, paid the secretary, and left.

I was disappointed and sad. All of my effort to try to get help had led to naught. And I was attacked all for nothing. My heart plummeted. And I vowed never to deal with attorneys again because it was all about the money and not correcting injustices.

CHAPTER NINETEEN

April entered with inviting sun and summoning in cordial boughs of warmth. Neighbors planted yellow wildflowers and the robins were landing a brief second or two on hanging baskets with songs of spring. With the crispness of a new day, I opened the windows and pushed back the curtains knowing that this would be a marvelous day – or at least I wanted it to turn out that way. In the kitchen, I turned over the calendar to the picture of a sunrise dawning of a new day. The freshness of a new season had brought a new outlook and new hope in solving the murder. In the back of my mind, I knew that some cases went for decades or were never solved at all, but I wouldn't accept that possibility. I was somewhat sore from the incident the day before, but I had resolved to take some pleasure in this day.

As my German cuckoo clock struck 10, my phone rang and after saying "hello," I waited for the caller but there was no sound.

I heard a rustling and an elderly lady said, "Maddie, is that you?" She had a hearing problem so she talked extra loud, and I had to hold the phone away from my ear because of the inflection of her voice penetrated my ear.

Hearing a frail and cracking voice, I said, "Yes, Granny Mildred," in ascending intonation.

"This is your granny in Batavia." Granny Mildred was my paternal grandmother and only one of my close relatives since my parents died in a car accident many years ago. She had always been there to comfort and support me any way she could. She had a keen acumen and a certain wit about her.

"Did I wake you?"

"Oh no, I was goin' to call you to see how your therapy has been with your leg.

Are you doing better now?"

"Yes, indeed, my leg is better. I was hobbling around but now I'm fine. Thank you so much for the card. Are you coming to visit this old biddy anytime soon?"

One part of me wanted to see her and another part wanted to stay here being caught up in this investigation.

Almost begging, she said, "I want to show you my flower bed that I have now and that I've been working on. I do have help planting 'cause when I get down on my knees, it's tough to get back up … so I pray to God that he gives me the strength and will to get back up again."

"That sounds like a metaphor for life." "What was that again honey? I didn't hear you."

"Nothin'. Let me think. How about this weekend? Are you busy on Saturday?"

"No, I'm here most days. At my age, there are few people I want to see and few places that I want to go."

"Don't say that. Eighty is not all that old by today's standards."

"Yeah, I guess. I feel it though."

"I know. Let's go to that tea house for lunch, my treat."

"I'd like that." Granny Mildred's spirits were lifting slightly and she said, "How about coming up around 11 and I'll make a reservation at noon.

"That's terrific."

Chuckling, she said, "I won't keep you all day 'cause I know that you'll want to get back to Cincy for your Saturday night date, and I'm sure you have a date with some handsome man. Tell me about him on Saturday."

Sounding like I was scolding a small child, I said, "Granny Mildred, I do *not* have a man in my life. . ."

"And why not?"

"Cause, 'cause ..." "Keep looking – don't tell me you're not interested, that'd be hogwash. He'll pop up like one of my petunias, sometimes in the darndest places."

"I'm pretending that I didn't hear that," I said.

Ignoring my last remark, Granny said, "I'll see you on Saturday at 11. Drive carefully. Love you."

"Love you." And I marked my calendar for Saturday doubting that I'd forget that date.

CHAPTER TWENTY

There was always something different in Saturday's mood. Psyching myself up for spending most of the day with Granny Mildred actually enlivened my spirits and I wanted to spend some time with her since she didn't have a lot going on down in Batavia. One small act of kindness to my granny by spending the day with her was one thing I could do, if only I could find something in my closet to wear. My walk-in closet was so packed with stuff it was hard to find anything to wear. I yanked out some capri pants, a blouse with a frilly collar, and some gold earrings. Brushing my hair back and slipping on some strappy sandals, I checked my appearance in the round mirror near the door. Satisfactory, but I needed a little makeup so I put on some lipstick.

Making my way down 275 was rough because of the bumper-to-bumper traffic, but I didn't let it bother me because I was determined to have a pleasant day. I stepped on the gas to pass cars lined up for the Montgomery and I-71 exits. My Mercedes was straining somewhat, and I flew by the cars to make good time. Getting close to Batavia, I merged onto the Gordon exit and down Peacock Road to Granny's home. Pulling up to her bungalow, I could see the old, familiar kelly green home with white shutters and an American flag by the front door. I walked up the cobblestone sidewalk along the meticulously cut yard. In the next yard, children were playing and chasing each other with water pistols. The front door was open but the screened door was still locked as I rang the doorbell. To the left side above my head was a wind chime and I brushed the chimes back and forth to make a melodious tinkling. Granny Mildred showed up at the door and unlocking the screen door, she said, "You made it," with a smile causing the long wrinkles to stretch across her face.

She limped on an unsteady leg as she shifted her weight from one foot to the other like a toddler learning to walk. She was wearing a light blue dress with intricate details of her embroidery, a dress that she had made herself. Her flat shoes hugged her large trunk legs. There was no division between her feet and trunk-like legs that were like two cylinders.

She gave me a kiss on the cheek and said, "Give me a hug sugar." She examined me like a biologist examining a specimen and said, "Are you eating enough?"

"Yeah, I'm eatin' plenty."

"That is a darling outfit, but, you know, handmade clothes are the best quality. Did you ever use the sewing machine that your mother left you?"

"No, I don't really have time to make my own clothes. Granny, no one sews anymore or does anything like that now."

Shaking her head indignantly, she said, "In my day, sewing and canning fruits and vegetable were skills that were required and valued."

"Today's skills for women are technology, business, and medicine and anything that can get them a solid job."

"Times change. Anyway, before we go into the house, I wanna show you my flower beds out back." We walked along a small path to the side of the house to a fence made of walnut brown planks and a gate that had a steel clasp wrapping around plastic cords. It was a small gate that separated the front and back yards.

I said, "Someone told me that entering Heaven through the narrow gate is something only few can do."

Without hesitation, she said, "That's from the Book of Matthew. Words to live by."

How she knew that was from Matthew off the top of her head, I didn't know, but I did want to know what she surmised from it.

"What exactly does that mean?"

"Maddie, dear, it means that so many people do things to mess up their lives. We can live by obedience and create our lives to make it the best that God wants for us, but few choose to really do what God intended. Life is precious . . . and short."

I was lost in deep thought. Walking through the rows of flowers and picking several here and there, she explained, "There is meaning and purpose in life if we have faith. Those who go through the narrow gate are always blessing what's in front of them, knowing that there is something better ahead – and blessing even the worst of times. It's faith that makes the impossible possible to endure."

"What is ahead? – hope and healing?"

"And a Heaven that we cannot imagine." We perused the magnificent and aromatic flowers, fruits, and vegetables all in neat rows. Granny Mildred said, "I try to look for five things every day that naturally occur and to be grateful for, like flowers, birds, and even the dog house over there. Gratitude keeps my heart young."

My emotions for some odd reason were getting the best of me, as I felt in between laughing and crying and looked up to an amethyst sky with golden rods of light shining down on Granny's silver hair.

Granny Mildred wobbled on her legs and she panted from only a few steps walking down the rows. She glanced at her watch. "Are you hungry?"

"Always hungry." And we took off in Granny's 60s Chevy at lightning speed down the Highway 32 east and onto Summit Avenue. Granny pulled up to the a sign that read, "Adelaide's Tea House," and there were people walking around an outside porch that stretched around an antebellum house with wrought iron table and chairs scattered under trees in the yard.

A young man dressed in black pants and a starched white shirt said, "What's your last name?"

Granny said, "It's under the name Pugh."

Scanning the reservation list, the server said, "It's here. Allow me to show you to your table." He sat us in the large room with a beautiful flower arrangement in the middle and linen napkins and silverware set perfectly on the table.

He asked, "What would you care to drink with your lunch?"

Granny said, "I'll have Earl Grey tea," and I told him that I'd have the same. He said, "Excellent, and you may help yourself to the buffet."

We got in line that went out the door and entering I could see people helping themselves to the buffet table, lavishly decorated with Italian figurines and crystal water vases. On silver and china platters were triangular finger sandwiches of every kind – cucumber, shrimp and ham salad, luscious salads, sweet bread, melon balls, and another table of cakes and cookies. The server came to our table and showed us the box of assorted teas. He poured the boiling water from a large silver tea pot and held the bottom with a linen cloth to shield her hands from the hot surface. We filled our plates and ate like British royalty at our elegant round table covered with a satiny pink tablecloth. When only a few crumbs remained on my plate, I reclined in my cushiony chair and rested my palms in my lap, I said, "Wow, gourmet food is good, like French food, you fill up on small portions with every bite of rich food."

Granny Mildred, embarrassingly picking her teeth with a toothpick said, "You look content. You haven't told me yet, what you've been up to in the Queen City?"

I couldn't help but scowl at what might be the beginning of twenty questions into my life and parts that shouldn't be broached at that moment. "Uh, I've been hunting for more lucrative, full-time teaching positions. . . ."

"A more lucrative position-- you should be grateful to have any job these days with so many people out of work." her pitch above the norm of guests around us.

"Sshh," I said softly, "You don't understand."

"What is it then that I don't understand?" Granny Mildred had a bewildered expression.

"It's complicated but I was threatened by a Saudi student who might have murdered a UC professor."

Granny raised her eyebrows and said, "I'm astonished. They should punish him by deporting him ASAP. You're telling me nothing has been done?"

"It's not that simple. Apparently it doesn't matter what is done to teachers or any instructors anymore especially if it's a paying student."

Granny Mildred said, "That disgusts me. Teachers should be respected – always."

"The problem is that the police can't do anything if they can't prove it with evidence. Even a Saudi national can get off scott free. The system supports the perpetrator."

"Unbelievable. There's no justice today. Nobody's responsible or held accountable."

"Unfortunately, that's true." I sensed that Granny really did get the situation was evident in her indignation, and it was a good conversation. We finished our tea and talked more about current events and the latest fashions.

Granny Mildred said, "Bright colors are in this year, aren't they?"

Agreeing, I said, "Bright colors are in – that's the fashion this year."

"What I wouldn't give to have a Coach handbag. Do you see that lady's Coach bag?"

Before I could see what she was seeing, my cell phone rang. "Excuse me, Granny, I have to take this call."

"Maddie, this is Mike Singleton, how are you doin' these days?"

"Fine. I'm out having lunch. What's up with the case?"

"We have finished the preliminary questioning of suspects, and boy, it's certainly been a drawn-out process."

"Do you have any prime suspect, or should I say suspects, now?" "Not yet, and it's tough for me to tell you that but we can't seem to pin down who was behind the murder."

"Nothing?" I said with obvious agitation.

"All of the students' alibis checked out and since it's April now, the trail has gotten cold. There's some evidence and slim chance that any other evidence will surface."

"After all of the money that I've been paying you and no answers. What evidence do they have?"

"I'm not comfortable with sharing that over the phone. Why don't you meet me at my office around 2, or 2:30, and we can discuss it then?"

"2:30 it is. See you then."

CHAPTER TWENTY-ONE

I realized that I had to get back to Cincinnati and find out what had materialized, if anything, and get to the bottom of what had transpired between all of the suspects and investigators. Completely dejected – alone in a pit – that's how I felt, but I knew one thing, that I wasn't staying in that pit forever.

Arriving at Mike's office, I rang the bell at the locked door. Mike approached and pushed open the door that was sticking even more and scraping to allow me to enter. His concerned expression did not bode well with me. Inside my eyes had to adjust to the dark hallway.

Mike said, "How's life been treatin' you?" That question seemed to trivialize why I was there.

I said, "I went to Batavia to visit my granny," which was irrelevant information. While picking up the papers off the chair so I could sit down, Mike made himself comfortable behind his desk and stretched his arms onto his desk as if he were a CEO about to give a conference.

Mike outlined the case. He said, "This is what we have. The crime scene photos in this envelope are gruesome and they don't show evidence per se. The coroner's report indicates that Loretta Bryson was killed with a heavy, blunt object. We don't know what it was but it inflicted enough of a blow to cause death."

"What about the office? Was there any evidence in the office – fibers, hairs, or fingerprints?"

"None – and that's a hindrance to solving the case. Any fibers or hairs found in the office still wouldn't link it to the murder."

Digging for any bit of evidence, I said, "Nothing else? But Agent Garrett found a so-called footprint?" I remembered Agent Garrett checking out my shoes at my front door.

"What do you mean by 'so-called'? It might be the heel of a shoe but there was a block mark on the floor, and if it is a woman's shoe, then that is even more confusing since we believe that a man delivered the blow."

Exasperated, I said, "Great. The murderer might have been a man or woman in stylish heels– that helps."

Mike said, "Or there might have been two people present – a man and a woman but just a theory."

I sighed deeply. "I assume you videotaped your questioning of the suspects? Is it possible for me to watch those?"

"Maddie, the other two agents and I did the questioning and we didn't find anything out of the ordinary or suspicious. Thousands of murders happen every year and they go unsolved."

Shaking my head back and forth in defiance, I said, "There's no way, no way that I'm letting this thing go – not until I get some answers. And that Saudi student will pay for his threats and murder, a senseless murder." I could feel my face reddening and beading sweat bullets.

Mike did not expect this strong of a response and leaning forward, he looked me in the eyes and said with a conciliatory tone, "We're not gonna stop until we solve this, for everyone's sake, and so the campus can be a safer place because there's a lot of fear among everyone."

"Good 'cause I'm not throwin' in the towel."

Mike said, "Why don't you give me a call in a couple of weeks and I'll give you another update."

I wrapped my arms around my bag which was on my stomach so my hands clutched my elbows. I felt my taser in my bag and said, "Oh yeah, do you have an extra battery for my taser and can you switch out the old one for me?"

"Sure. Let me see your taser. I'll have to check in the back supply closet to see if I have it in stock. If so, I can change it for you."

"I feel 100 percent more secure with it."

"Oh I understand."

Unzipping my bag, I handed him my purple taser pointing it downward.

He opened the lever and said, "Yep, that's a dead battery." He exited the room and I cranked my head to follow him through the double doors down the hall. For some crazy reason, I ran around his desk and started looking frantically through his desk drawers to find the videotapes. It was such a mess but in the bottom, I found a box and they were labeled, "Bryson Murder – interviews," and each tape was dated. I was in the middle of thumbing through the tapes when Mike appeared in the doorway holding the taser. I jumped off the chair.

"Looking for something?"

I said, "You scared the b-Jesus outta me."

"You found the interviews I presume? If you wanna watch them that bad, we can watch every boring one."

"It's OK?"

"Well, they're evidence so they can't leave my possession."

"What are you saying exactly? That we gotta watch them together?"

"Yeah, if you don't mind me hangin' out in the same room?" He almost chuckled.

I said, "Whatever. But can we at least be comfortable?"

With a smile, Mike said, "Oh I see. You mean not in this disorganized mess?"

"I didn't say that. I can't believe that I'm asking you over but my home is private and we won't be disturbed."

"Oh I see. Date night and a video."

"Yeah. If you're free this evenin'. See you around 7."

"I'm free and I'll bring the pizza." I was ambivalent about this proposition, but I'd invested too much in this case to not know every detail of the evidence.

CHAPTER TWENTY-TWO

Later that afternoon, I went home and took a power nap in order to be alert and ready for a long evening of videos and working on the case. I knew that I had to be alert to observe every comment, every gesture and every detail that could give the murderer away. At 7:30 or so, Mike showed up with pizza, beer, and the box of videos. He was overloaded with stuff in his arms so I grabbed the videos so he'd only have the pizza and beer to carry up.

He followed me up the stairs and said, "Sorry I'm late, but a detective's work never has a regular schedule."

I said, "Yeah, with all of the car chases and shoot outs I guess it's hard to stay on a regular schedule."

"I rarely have anything that exciting . . . just run of the mill days like parents who don't have custody of their kids and take them across state borders and I have to get them back or other cases like insurance fraud..."

"Oh, that's an ordinary day?"

"Most days, yeah." I placed the videos down on the footstool and went in the kitchen, and he put the pizza and beer on the counter.

I suggested, "Do you wanna eat now – I'm starved."

"Yeah, I'm ready to dig in."

I got out plates and glasses and we both got our pizza and opened up the beer and poured it in the tall glasses. We moved around the kitchen like we were in synch with each other. It was almost eerie that for a moment we mirrored each other the way married couples do when they know each other's thoughts and respond in using the same short responses that happen naturally, without much thought process. Mike sat on the sofa against the wall, and I made myself comfortable in the large chair in the middle of the room.

I said, "Show time, I suppose."

Mike said, "Unless you wanna watch a movie."

I said, "No, No, don't be ridiculous. I've been waiting to analyze these videos."

"The first person that we interviewed is Paul Bennett."

I laughed. "It looks more like Paul Bunyan. Wow, he has some head of hair."

He had a mound of tangled hair on his head that looked like a place that a small animal could get lost in. A muscular, 40-ish man with a scraggly beard sat in the chair which he covered with his massive body. His bushy, brown eyebrows rounded his eyes and his suntanned face was worn and weathered. His flannel shirt and camper-style cargo pants showed his bulging physique. He looked as if he could play a Grizzly Adams if he had been wearing overalls, boots, and carried an ax.

Mike said, "This guy, despite his appearance, was very sincere in his answers and we didn't suspect him because he cooperated and didn't have the opportunity to murder Loretta since he had an alibi."

In the video, Agent Nelson and Garrett and Mike were in a semi-circle while Paul sat in front of the desk. Distracted by his appearance, I didn't hear all of the questions that Agent Nelson was asking him.

Agent Garrett was uttering the usual questions. "How do feel about your job? Where were you the night that Ms. Bryson was murdered?" It was as if he were reciting a script in which he expected all of the answers.

Mike interjected to ask me, "How many of these instructors and people we are interviewing did you know from your teaching time there?"

I said, "Not many. They had such a high turnover that I don't recognize any of them. They might have transferred from another English department just to keep the program and class schedule going."

Next, a video of a pretty woman flashed on the screen.

Mike said, "Her name is Adrianna Trudy. She seems to be from a *privileged* class if you know what I mean." Adrianna wore a slightly sheer pink blouse and she had pearl barrettes that pulled back her blond hair and her pink lipstick accented her overly white teeth. Her makeup was immaculate.

I said, "Oh I remember working with her. She was always going out to ritzy clubs with her boyfriend and attending concerts."

Mike said, "She was attending a fundraiser for the ALS Society that night so I doubt we could consider her."

"What questions was she asked?" I asked.

"Same ol' questions. She had a rather fake smile, smug but she appeared truthful."

I shook my head and said, "She always swayed grades for students that she liked, especially students from Brazil where she had cousins. Favoritism, yes, but murder, no way. Who's next?"

Mike said, "You'll be interested in this. This is Fahad Faruq. He was a real character. I think the agents had to call him a couple of times to track him down. Seems this guy spends a lot of time at the hookah cafe."

"Yeah, that's because when you have something to hide, you don't want to be tracked down and questioned."

Fahad was a Saudi Arabian student with stringy, black hair and a black mustache. He was short, and his voice was hoarse from smoking strong cigarettes, and his clothes looked like he slept in them. He wore a military style jacket and a cap that made his long hair stick out at the bottom. His puke green tennis shoes looked strangely out of place with the rest of his clothes. I turned up the volume.

Agent Garrett took the lead in the questioning. "Sir, what is your name? Where are you from and how long have you been living in the U.S?"

"I've been living here for two years, and I attend the university." "What's your address?"

"Address is McPherson Street. Can't remember the number. Will call my friend."

Agent Nelson said, "No, that's not necessary. We want to ask you more about your classes here." The agents and Mike realized that there might be some problems with communication and began to enunciate their words. It sounded really unnatural.

Agent Nelson said with more emphasis, "How long, how many weeks or months have you been here in Cincinnati?"

Crossing his arms, Fahad said, "I'm here for about four months. I arrived in December and I started classes in January. I have two roommates. They are from Saudi Arabia, too."

Mike said, "Did you ever talk to Loretta Bryson?"

"Yeah, I talked to her about my work. I had trouble with writing. Yeah, she helped me with tutor on campus."

Mike continued, "Did you pass your classes?"

Defensive, he said, "No, I didn't pass all classes... one 'bout culture. I had to go to court, so I missed too much classes."

Mike, with a smirk, said, "You missed too many classes, not too much."

"Ah, yes, too many classes. Anyway, I have to retake the class."

Agent Garrett said, "Were you OK with taking the class?"

Fahad said, "Yeah, I need to learn English for my work at the university." "And what is that going to be?"

Fahad said proudly, "I go to study chemical engineering so I can go back to Saudi Arabia and work in my country."

Agent Nelson said, "Where were you the night of Ms. Bryson's murder?"

"Uh, that night, I go, I mean, I went with my roommate to hookah cafe and then we went home."

"Please write down your friend's name and his information on this card," said Agent Garrett.

"Is my friend in trouble?"

Agent Garrett said, "No, but we just have to check out who was on the campus camera and make sure that they check out."

Fahad hesitates in taking the card and writes very slowly stopping after each word as if he were trying to recall the information.

Agent Garrett took the card and said, "That's it for now. We'll call you if we need anything further."

Fahad looked confused and leaves rather bewildered.

Mike was sound asleep and I threw a throw blanket on him as he peacefully slept off the worries of the day. I'm feeling more awake than ever and I watched a few more interviews. But I kept eyeing the list of suspects that Mike had in his bag. Temptation got the better of me and I eased it out of his bag and as he was waking up, I slipped it under the seat cushion.

Mike awoke and said, "Oh man, what time is it?"

"It's very late."

Fumbling to put on his shoes back on and put on his coat, he said, "I'll be back tomorrow around 7 or so, and we can watch more then."

Feeling that I had something real to go on, I stayed up late reading over the names on the list.... all with no knowledge that I had stolen the list of suspects.

CHAPTER TWENTY-THREE

Pages and pages of scribbled note and lists of names. The next to the last page listed the Office of Saudi Arabian Education Institute in Washington, DC that sponsored the students all over the country. They paid generous amounts of scholarship money for students to get their education. There were contact names, numbers, and emails and a list of students. Some of the students' names had checks beside them. I made myself comfortable in my big cozy chair and read down the list.

Scrolling down the list, I looked for familiar names among the last names which were

Abadi
Alqahtani
Al Toukri
Assaf
Basara
Faruq√
Hakimi
Katani
Moghadan
Said
Shamun
Wasem

I noticed that the only name checked was Faruq and that left me wondering why there hadn't been more activity into their investigation of the Saudi students. I didn't recognize most of the names on the list except Alqahtani and Faruq of course. Why wasn't Alqahtani one of the first to be questioned? It didn't make any sense to me if they knew that someone else was involved. After tucking away the list in my desk, I thought about how I might use these students to help me solve the case.

The next morning while thinking about how I could use this list of names, I remembered how Mike had told me that Faruq and his buddies spent quite a bit of time at the hookah cafe. An ingenious plan flashed into my mind. The plan was to pay a student, or students, to go into the hookah cafe and listen in on their conversations. That seemed like a daunting task but there's a lot of "talk" that goes on in those hookah cafes like what stupid people start saying when they get drunk in bars. The FBI probably had someone who spoke Arabic and could gather information from any of the Middle Eastern students. The only problem was that hookah cafes were an experience for men only. Women didn't smoke hookah so how could they be spied on? I don't know but I had to call Mike – and confess about taking the list.

My phone rang. Mike said angrily, "Did you take any papers from my bag last night?" Oh no, he knows already.

I was shaking because he was irate. "Yeah, I sort of wanted to get a handle on . . ."

"A handle on what? Something that you have no business reading?"

"I was working on . . ."

"*You're* not working on anything. You are outside the scope of this. Do you understand?" Mike was ballistic.

Scolded like a child, I said, "I understand. I thought that the agents could send someone into the hookah cafe and get some information.

That's all."

"It's *not* your job to be planning how to solve this case."

"OK. I got it."

Mike realized that he had gotten his point across, and he simmered down. He said, "Why don't you go out with some of your friends and take in a movie or something."

I felt talked down to, but what could I do? Agreeing, I said, "Yeah, that's probably something I'd like."

"Yeah, I told you before that I'd let you know something when I find out."

"Thanks. And I will send these papers back –pronto. I promise." And I hung up.

****

Before I decided to completely "hand over" this case to Mike and the agents, I hatched one last plan to get some answers on my own. I'd heard that the University of Cincinnati had bonfires at certain times of the year, and I surmised that I might be able to talk with some students about what rumors were circulating about possible suspects. So I made a trip down to the west end of campus near the park where students were huddled around a bonfire that was sending streams of dashing flames with flickers of sparks that danced high into the air. Every so often a student would jump backwards from a loud pop and snap from a flame that had gone horizontally and not upward. The night air was cool and the students were wearing thick sweaters and flannel shirts, raggedy split jeans, and Bengals caps. Some sneaky students were trying to conceal beer and liquor that they had underneath their jackets but the smell was too pungent along with the potent cigarette smoke. Not only were students there but some people who lived in the neighborhood who had wandered over to watch the bonfire and witness the university spirit. Those people were off my radar for questions as they probably wouldn't know as much as the students. A group of about six or seven students toward the inner part of the lot was taking charge of the bonfire. They were very carefully monitoring the bonfire and the crowd with an occasional warning to stand back and to set more wood on the fire. I wanted to get over to them to ask them some questions, but some of the students who were drinking would bump me to the side practically pushing me down. As I pushed back, a guy turned around and gave me a psychotic stare as if he were asking me why I was being the aggressor. To diffuse the situation, I said, "Oh sorry, I stumbled," and he didn't say anything but put his arm around his girlfriend and continued to blow cigarette smoke into the air. Waiting for the excitement of the bonfire to simmer down, I made my way close to two students, a male and female, who were passing supplies onto the others.

I said, "Hi, nice night. Could I ask you two a couple of questions about the murder that took place on campus – Loretta Bryson?"

The male student, perturbed, said, "Are you from the police or newspaper?"

I said, "I'm just helping the detectives to help them solve this case so everyone can feel a little safer on campus."

Amenable to my questions, the female student said, "Sure. What do you want to know?"

I asked, "Who are the students saying was behind the murder? Do they talk about anyone who might have gotten in the building and murdered Ms. Bryson?"

The female student said, "Well it's not talked about that much now, but there were some students in my psychology class who said that a Chinese student was the murderer."

"A Chinese student? What's his or her name?"

The female student continued. "It's Lila Chang. She was always freakin' out about her grades and having a meltdown when she didn't get the grade that she thought she deserved, so she would . . . ."

The male student interrupted, "Hey, not *all* the students thought Lila would do that. It was just a rumor." He looked at the female student with an air of condescension, and he pulled his cap tighter on his head and went over to the fire to stoke some flames that billowed up making the surrounding students put out their hands to grab some warmth.

The female student said, "Well, that's what I heard – that Lila and some of her freaky friends were plotting something. But I guess it could've been anyone these days."

I had one last question for the female student. I asked her, "Why do you think your friend would defend Lila? He seemed to be on her side?"

The female student said, "I think that he was having some problems in some of his classes, and Lila helped him out. She was the guru in some classes. But she expected the instructors to give her better grades and she was always partying and not getting anything done on time. So she fumed all the time."

I thanked the female student for her help and left, intending on calling Mike the next day with the information. And to see if he would even talk to me.

CHAPTER TWENTY-FOUR

The following day I had to tutor at school and was not in the mood for it. At school, I thought about the list of suspects – what was lying?

At school, a teacher would occasionally ask me a question and I was in another world.

I had to say several times, "I'm sorry. I was thinking about something else."

And I was. I was consumed by whatever outcome might be to the case.

Emad. He was a student from Jordan brought his paper up to me and gave me an intimidating look. He definitely wasn't backing down from what he wanted.

"Ms. Hauck, I deserve a better grade on this writing." He handed me his essay with a contemptible look.

I refused to take the paper but I could see that I wrote a "72" at the top. I said, "What grade did you expect because some parts are incomprehensible."

Slapping the paper on the desk, he demanded, "I deserve at least an 80. There's nothing wrong with it. It's a good paper."

A good paper? He earned that grade and I wasn't budging on it. I said, "That's what you earned and if you want to re-write it, I could give you several points."

Furious and spitting from his angry words, Emad said, "No, I'm not rewriting anything. It's fine like it is."

He snatched up the paper and left the room. Calm and cool on the exterior, I was shaking in fright. And I was fed up with his recalcitrant ways. Just a spoiled brat. I took out my key and locked the classroom door, in fear that he would return and get more violent. Waiting for him to leave, I opened up my desk drawer to grade some papers. After an hour and not concentrating, I got my things together and decided to leave. I heard my supervisor, Kristen Kreutz's. Her stern voice annoyed and startled me at the same time. She was a heavy-set woman with frosted hair, and her polyester suits made a swishing sound when she walked. She was mid-thirties and had been supposedly put in this position by her ambitious and overzealous father who had donated money to the school.

"Ms. Hauck, I'll need to see you in my office."

"Would it be possible to talk later? I have a dentist's appointment."

"No, this cannot wait. Follow me."

Ms. Kreutz led me down the hallway to her office. She slammed the door and the loudness made me wince.

Her shrill voice caused a shooting pain in my ear. In a high pitch, she said, "I had a visit today from Emad today. He was quite upset over his grade. He thought that you should've given him a better grade."

"I gave him what he earned. If he wants to sit down with me, I can explain how he can do better with . . ."

Ms. Kreutz was on a verbal rampage, bullying and harassing me. She said,

"No, that won't do. We have *paying* students here. That's how you keep your job, from their *tuition*, so I suggest you get out your grade book and curve his grade up."

Speechless, I took out my grade book and started erasing, trying hold back the tears in the corners of my eyes. Ms. Kreutz was standing over me and hectoring me with her hands on her hips. I was defenseless. And crushed.

She said, "You obviously don't understand the *culture* of rich people. They get what they want. That's how the world works."

My throat felt swollen like it had a baseball-sized lump and I only muttered, "Yes, ma'am."

Opening the door, she said, "Now run along to your appointment."

After fixing it, Ms. Kreutz opened the door and I left walking out to the parking lot with my hand over my mouth feeling nauseous – and in utter disgust. I hit the gas with a screech trying to beat the stop light. Enough of tutoring for one day. I envisioned her having a massive heart attack, collapsing to the floor, and dying an agonizing death. . . . And I thought that was what she deserved.

CHAPTER TWENTY-FIVE

April 15, 2013

April showers might bring some gorgeous May flowers, but here in Ohio, the spring brings allergies and sinus difficulties. Rustling winds settle pollen on my dining table. With the overhead light shining on the glass, the yellow particles clouded over the candles and Polish pottery plates. I wiped the pollen from the glass ware. My head felt congested and I took some medicine before lying down propping myself up to alleviate any midnight asthma spell. An hour or two later, I drifted off into a nightmare. In my frightening dream, I found myself lying in a dungeon with coal-black walls on all four sides. Scared, I got up and pounded on the wall in front of me and with no light, I slid along the wall in a maze searching for a way out. After an endless episode of yelling for help and fists reddened and bruised from beating on the walls, I lie back down on the cold, unforgiving floor. Two figures emerged and scooping me up underneath my arms, they begin to drag me to an unknown place – I am doomed as fires surround the gravel-lined road. In the distance, I see a building with the number 2-1-8 and the two figures arguing violently. In a desperate attempt to stop, I pray to God to save me .....and then I wake up.... my heart beating fast and realizing that I am safe and sound at home. It is silent in my room except for the tick-tock of the wall clock and the neighbor's flag whipping in the wind. My mother had always told me that powerful dreams have meaning. She always told me, "Maddie, Pay attention to your dreams. They're powerful. They're new information and they always tell you something that is buried way down in your subconscious." And mama was right. It was the early morning hours of April 15, 2013 and I had an uneasy feeling about the day.

I felt sick from my allergies and wanted to wrap a blanket around myself and sleep from the after effects of an antihistamine. Despite sniffling and sneezing, I set off down Vine Street to a church where I did volunteer tutoring two days a week. This morning, I drove extra carefully down the street where blinding sunlight caused a glare off the chrome bumper of the truck in front of me. I made my way down Seymour Avenue to the church with its ornate towers like spires jutting so high that you had to crack your neck uncomfortably upward to see the very top. I pulled into the parking lot taking my bag with my easy English workbook and English-Spanish dictionary. The small Sunday school room felt chilly. It was cluttered with books, toys, and stuffed animals all crammed onto old shelves. There were six students, four women and two men, waiting at the little round table that had munchkin size chairs. They were all smiling and eagerly waiting for me. They were: Maria, Rosa, Luz, Mario, and Pilar. It was 1:58 pm.

We were supposed to start at 2 pm so I said, "Lo siento. (Sorry) I'll be early next time," and they just grinned from ear to ear. I took my book out of my bag and we played games with command words such as "Open the book" and "Close the door." Next, we looked at a page in the book of medical terms and learned how to say *head-ache* with a "k" sound and not *head-aitch*. After the session was over, I hurried home to find out the latest news. Pulling up to my home hit the brakes. My breathing was labored and wheezing and my bags bustled as I climbed the stairs upstairs. I dropped the bags on the counter and turned on the TV. There in the middle of the marathoners were broadcasters, some with tears, giving an account of the time and how many people were taken to hospitals – and the horrible news – the toll of hurt and killed was climbing. Was this another incident from terrorists? I called Mike Singleton on my speed dial. I hoped that what had transpired before with us had blown over, and besides, he was still being paid to work on this case. I heard a distant static and silence between scratchy noises like the reception from the 1970s two-way radio sets.

"Mike, are you there?" I asked with tearful sobbing. Static and electricity and then a brief lull.

"Yeah, I'm here. I'm in Indiana on assignment. I'm guessing that you heard about the bombing in Boston?"

Subdued, I said, "Do you think that our case is related to what happened in Boston?" I thought that I had lost the connection and wondered if I was asking a question with no answer. . . . well, not yet.

"Gee, I haven't the foggiest. I mean, who knows? There are terrorists in every city."

"When is this going to end?" I said with frustration.

Mike didn't know what to say. After a pause, then he said, "Maddie, there's nothing we can do until we get more. I know it's hard to relax but we'll talk later. Gotta run. I'm taping someone on an insurance fraud case." End of conversation.

Even though Mike hung up, I was grateful that he was available and there. But all the while I was learning to cope with disasters by being aware of what was going on around me and knowing that we were under God's control.

CHAPTER TWENTY-SIX

Despite promising myself that I would no longer depend on sedatives for relief, I was back on medication again. Pounding heart and nervousness prevented me from any deep sleep. I couldn't help it but I was back on the meds, but I told myself that this was worse, much worse than anything before. On all TV stations, the haunting scenes of bloody people hobbling and stretched out on the pavement resembled a war zone. I couldn't get the images out of my head so I turned off the TV and rested in a cool bath. The "what-ifs" were overwhelming me. What if this is a Saudi? What if they don't catch him and he sets another bomb? Whoever was responsible needed to pay for this.

With nerves that finally succumbed to rest, I dozed off in the evening hours when the phone rang.

Timidly, Mike said, "Maddie, were you resting? Thought I'd check on you."

"No, no only resting my eyes. You sound drained."

"Uh, I've had some setbacks with that case that I'm on now, that's all. I know that the bombing today must've really upset you."

"I know that it was a Saudi behind it," I shrieked.

"Maddie, we don't know that for sure.... yet. The FBI is on it, and believe me, they're gonna get who was behind all of these horrendous . . ."

Crack, bam, boom.. Thumping. A screech. . . then silence. My heart skipped a beat. "Mike, are you still there?" I yelled. Rustling and a thump. "Mike!" A few seconds later. . . .

"I'm here. I'm staking out someone in this abandoned part of Indianapolis; er . . . there's gunfire every hour."

"I'm so *worried* about you."

After the Boston bombing tragedy, I could not bear for Mike to get hurt or killed. "You've gotta get out of there. It's not worth your life. . ."

"I'm almost done – I've, I've got what I needed," and he sighed deeply. His soothing voice soothed me like cool water on a parched hot day. I had grown attached to Mike with his reassuring ways and he had become a friend to me in this crazy world. So I was on a mission of how we would find Loretta's murderer.

****

Why is it that everything in the morning doesn't seem so bad? Amid the violence on TV, spring time had opened up the warm blue skies. Yellow buttercups blossomed as seasons were turning. My favorite spot to meditate this time of year was Winton Woods Park where the lake, campgrounds, and walkways were an idyllic place to find one-ness and connect to nature. The walkway stretched 1.5 miles around the lake and canoers, paddle boats, and motor boats bobbed on the water in peaceful repose. Tourists leisurely walked along and over the bridges, away from the cares of the world. I wanted to dispose of all of the bad that was infiltrating me like the penetrating stench from a sewer on a humid day. On the sidewalk, I overlooked the lake and stepped onto the track and began running . . . running my heart out in an effort to purge all of the evil that cloaked me and weighed me down with heaviness. Sprinting for the finish line. It all broke my soul... but only for the time being.

After jogging several times around the lake, I leaned over allowing the sweat to trickle off my forehead, onto my ears, and down to the ground. Exhaling and puffing for air, I wore myself out and staggered over to a shaded tree and a water fountain. Leaning over, I dunked my head underneath and pulled my shirt over my face to wipe away the sweat. Under the maple tree, I saw the view and the motionless vista – an inviting postcard – a snapshot of how we should live in harmony with the world – an ever-flowing world in constant change. With the winds picking up, I took one last sprint across the final bridge back to my car. Ready to get back to the task again.

It was almost like a routine now with Mike showing up with the tapes. The only difference was that it was staying lighter outside at this time of year, so the days were longer. A couple of kids were outside playing basketball. I closed the sliding glass door to black the banging ball against the backboard and sidewalk.

Mike rang the bell, and seeing his hands empty, I said, "Did you bring food?"

He said, "I'm not feelin' that hungry."

"Oh, well, if you do get hungry, I can run out and get some food."

"Don't worry about it. I doubt that I'll be here that long." I didn't know exactly what he meant, but I took the videos and hit the Play button. I wasn't sure why Mike wasn't his usual self, but I wasn't paying attention.

Mike said, "Oh yeah. There was a development today about some possible cover-up at the university. Some students were paying for grades."

"What? Say that again. I thought that you said . . ."

Mike said, "The police are finding out about some students who were in some scheme with teachers to get grades by paying a hefty price."

"You just thought to tell me this now."

Mike, nonchalant, said, "Until they can prove it, no one goes to jail."

"Saudi students, I know it. It's spelled out all in front of them. What more do they need?"

"It's possible but it could be any student or students. There are a lot of students out there from wealthy families that think that they can beat the system."

"Don't you think it all points to the Saudi students?"

"I really don't know. But they do wanna know if it has anything to do with the murder. And an abduction."

"An abduction? What next?"

Mike said, "The Cincinnati Police are investigating some Saudi students for an apparent abduction."

"An abduction?"

"Yeah, a Saudi student asked a female teacher to come to his house to tutor him and his friend. He told her that his family would be there and they would have a big dinner with kabsa, the chicken dish. He lured her there and then he and his friend kept her there and wouldn't let her go. She somehow got away by asking them if they could go outside and have a drink, and then she took off running for her car."

My mouth dropped open as I couldn't contain my disbelief. "What a horror story. Thankfully, she got away. From arson to abduction, those Saudis seem to be behind a lot. Just a matter of time before they have this murder pinned on them."

Mike was stretched out, and he was probably getting as tired of this as I was. The next interviewee was Patrick Gladstone. He was slim and anemic. His thinning hair atop his bald head made his head appear abnormally large and round. His bulging eyes looked as if he were emphasizing every word. He had a quiet demeanor and his wrinkled polo shirt was only half-way tucked in.

In the video, Mike asked Patrick, "How were you and Ms. Bryson getting along while she was your supervisor? Did you have any problems working with her?"

Patrick said, "Ms. Bryson didn't approve of my unconventional methods of teaching. I *wasn't* following what I was supposed to be teaching."

"What were *your* methods of teaching that conflicted with hers?"

Patrick's hesitated slightly as he formulated his answer. "I, uh, uh, taught from a Biblical standpoint. . . . but only *sometimes.*"

Agent Nelson said, "Didn't that make some Muslims and some non-religious students uncomfortable?"

Defensive, Patrick said, "I'm so tired of not being able to express *my* views in the classroom. If anyone wants to talk about Islamic views, then it's OK, but when mentioning anything Christian, then everyone is offended by it."

Mike, in the heat of questioning, said, "Was Ms. Bryson upset with this?"

Patrick shot back. "If she was upset, then she allowed it and to heck with any other students. They'll just have to get with it and adapt to whatever an instructor wants to do in class."

Both agents and Mike were scribbling notes quickly and Agent Nelson said, "Tell us where you were on the night of Ms. Bryson's murder."

Patrick's face grew ashen and he looked down and said, "That night I was at the UC hospital with my wife and baby. Our baby was diagnosed with heart disease, and he was very ill, but he's recovering now."

Agent Garrett said, "Is there anything else that you'd like to add – anything that you need to tell us?"

Upset, Patrick said, "It's been very painful for me and it's my fault for staying on campus so much but I was finishing up the semester and I had to get the grades and paperwork done. I should've been home with my sick child." Gently sobbing, he added, "I am struggling to be a husband, father, and instructor and it's been tough. . ." Looking down, he said, "I've had to moonlight at a bar at night to support my Chinese wife and baby. She wants her master's degree and I had to make some money to help her. It's just been tough."

Agent Nelson said, "We have you on the video camera before the power went out and all surveillance went dead. It shows you leaving around the time of the murder." Wiping away tears, Patrick said, "I was leaving because I hadn't got my work done. I told you that. I wish that I had but . . ."

Agents Nelson and Garrett told Patrick to take a few minutes to recollect himself and then he is dismissed.

Feeling sullen and sympathetic, I said, "Gosh, that guy doesn't fit the profile. He might have taught unconventionally but he didn't have the opportunity."

Taking a large gulp of soda, Mike said, "Yeah, the agents saw him on a tape leaving the building and campus but he's not a suspect. Only a guy who juggled things to get it all done. Not a prime suspect."

Definitely a person who had a run-in with a superior but his body language didn't depict someone who was violent – but what did I know? An exception always exists.

CHAPTER TWENTY-SEVEN

There was a blank screen and then a bright light flashed before the picture came into focus. Mike and I watched it, intent on scrutinizing the next interview.

Mike said, "You gotta see this next woman. We got our questions over with pronto 'cause she's the type of teacher that no one could put anything over on. Just take a look at this woman."

Next was an older woman in her early 60s who strutted in the room with a swaying of her wide curvy hips and a don't-mess-with-me attitude. She was wearing a tight, short black skirt that showed her large calves and she had a low-cut tiger print sweater what showed her bosomy figure. Her spiked heels clicked on the floor and her gaudy, dangling earrings and multiple gold bracelets made her jingle with every move. She had tight blond curls, an over-powdered face, and fake-looking blushed cheeks. Her smoking reflected in her teeth that had yellowed, and a strong tobacco odor emanated from her. She stared at all three men with a perturbed look and pulled her chair back making the men wonder if they should've gotten her chair for her.

Frustrated, she said, "I filled out the card with the information," and slapped it down on the table. "I have to teach a class in 30 minutes so I hope this is very brief."

Ian took the card and said, "Wanda, tell us about your teaching career, how long you have taught here, and any other pertinent information about the night of Ms. Bryson's murder."

Wanda spoke with a thick New Jersey accent. Condescendingly, she said, "I have been teaching English at UC for 25 years and I have an outstanding career – I've published over 50 articles and am known nationwide in my field.

"What about the night of the murder?" asked Mike.

"That night I was at Macy's with my daughter who was visiting from Chicago. She works as a state relations coordinator and we were buying last-minute gifts for family and friends."

"Were there any conflicts between you and Ms. Bryson?" Wanda rolled her eyes and stiffened her back in defiance. Her patience for questions was running out and it was obvious to all in the room.

She said, "I had asked Loretta for a raise since my husband has had some financial problems with his business so I asked for a raise a few months early."

"Did she give you the raise?"

"No way would she give me the money early. Are you kidding me? The higher-ups never appreciated anything the instructors did, no matter how hard we worked. It was never good enough." She put her hand over her eyebrow and said, "Is there any way you could dim that light in my eyes? It's giving me a headache."

Mike said, "I'm sorry but it has to be bright for the video-- to see your features clearly."

Agent Garrett said, "If you could bring us some of the receipts of your purchases, just so we can verify your whereabouts that night … we'd appreciate that."

Irritated, Wanda said, "Are you serious? Hassling me for receipts, how ridiculous. But if that's what you need, I'll bring them by tomorrow, same time." She took out a cigarette and held it up between her long, manicured nails and said, "Now if you'll excuse me, I'm preparing for class and I'd like to take my smoke break now."

The agents and Mike shrugged in compliance and Agent Nelson said, "Thank you for your time," as Wanda stomped out the room and huffed in annoyance as she exited.

I cut off the video and said to Mike, "Wow, that's one woman no one wants to mess with."

"Yeah, she's a tough broad. Can you imagine being a student in her class? I wouldn't want to show up without my homework – that'd be too much grief for anyone."

"Yeah, she's tough, but respected. Who's next?"

I was getting started. Mike slumped down on the sofa, and I sat glued to the screen.

Mike said, "I think there's one more video for the day."

"Who's that?"

"She's a 50-ish, Native American woman... very spiritual."

An olive-skinned woman with an oval, oily face entered the room. She had jet black hair pulled tightly back, and she sat slightly askew to the camera. She wore a rust-colored linen blouse with turquoise embroidery. She had a silver emblem on a chain that fell on her cleavage. Her plain features and soft-spoken voice were evident with the first words that she uttered.

We both watched as Mike said, "How are you today?"

"I'm well, Thank you." "Tell us, Faye, how was your relationship with Ms. Bryson?"

"Ms. Bryson and I were on good terms. She was a good person."

Her words sounded rehearsed and routine as if she someone had prompted her beforehand.

"Where were you the night of her murder?"

"I was babysitting for the people in my neighborhood. Some of the kids come over to play with my grandchild."

"And do you know of any of your colleagues who had problems with Ms. Bryson?"

"As far as I know, Ms. Bryson was well-liked by everyone," she said with an eerie smirk.

Skeptical, Ian said, "You mean that you don't know of even one teacher or student that *didn't* like Ms. Bryson?"

"Uh, no, the only instructor that had a problem with her was Madison Hauck." Mike tried to remain stone-faced as the agents looked askance at him.

Ian continued. "What was the problem?"

"Uh, I don't know exactly. She's the only person that I could think of who could do such a horrendous thing. They were arguing over grades and grade changing."

I was infuriated at seeing a former colleague implicate me. My temper got the best of me.

Furiously, I yelled, "Oh, my God. What a liar! That I murdered someone." I shut the video off. Wondering why there was no reaction from Mike, I noticed that he was fast asleep.

The video of Faye was cold and calculating. How she tried to pin the murder on me was an indication of something more, some other plot. I was convinced of that. I knew that she could very well be the murderer.

CHAPTER TWENTY-EIGHT

The videos of all of the suspects were largely unproductive in turning up anything. Now I understood why Mike had warned me that viewing all of them might not be worth my time but I plunged ahead. Examining every hand gesture, every pitch, and every word was wearing on me. After Mike dropped off to sleep, I played back portions of the videos scrutinizing them as if I were a body language expert and wondering if any other forensics tied the murderer to the scene. Taking a break, I turned off the videos and went out on the balcony to get some fresh air. The spring air was blowing and nights were shorter with more sunlight. And that only registered to me that there were more daylight hours to go down to campus to survey who was coming and going near the scene of the murder – and that's all it meant to me.

Nudging Mike, I said, "Hey, you fell asleep," I was bothered by his lack of interest.

Blinking and drooling, Mike said, "Man, oh man, am I wiped out." He finally widened his eyes and said, "Sorry, I'd better be on my way," and he half-way stumbled down the stairs saying, "I'll call you tomorrow."

And that was the end of the evening. He left without telling me when we would get together again, and that was huge. Were we going to continue on this path of trying to find the murderer? He revved up his car and barreled down the hill to the corner. Playing a detective in real life reminded me of a lunch box that I had in the first grade – a lunch box with a female detective bug-eyed with a magnifying glass. She wore a chestnut brown cape and military-style boots. I wanted to be like her solving crimes and getting the bad guy. But real life wasn't like that at all. I understood now the hard work. So much for any glamor. And so much for playing Maddie the Detective.

****

It was 7:30 the next morning and I overslept. I was weak and trembling from dehydration. My head ached and I sneezed and coughed for the first five minutes after waking.

Calling Myra, she answered on the first ring, "Hello," in a sleepy voice.

In a scratchy and hoarse voice, I said, "Myra, this is Maddie, I'm gonna need some extra time this morning to get myself together. I'm so sick and I'm gonna drive myself to school so I don't keep you waiting this morning."

Myra said, "Are you sure that you can make it today? You should stay and drink some fluids, or if you're that sick, see a doctor."

"I can make it today, but it'll take me a little longer to get dressed and get there. Go ahead and I'll be there later."

"OK, but let me know if you need anything."

"Thanks so much. I wish that you could call that witch Ms. Kreutz for me. I am *not* in the mood to call her but I have to."

"Yeah, go ahead and get it over with. I'll see you later."

"Yeah, thanks, I appreciate it." And calling the office, I decided to leave a message on the answering machine that I'd be late for tutoring today. That's one way to avoid dealing with a control freak.

After showering, taking some cold medicine, and eating some toast, I felt like I could muster through the day. The morning was long and I squeezed some lemon into a cup of hot tea, sipping on it to alleviate the hoarseness. When someone spoke to me, it was as if my lips said the words, but there was no sound. In the afternoon, with meds wearing off and teaching a lesson to several students, I felt shaky and feverish. A spring cold had gotten the best of me, and during a reading lesson, I casually moved toward the windows to get a breath of fresh air. I pulled the lever and turning it clockwise several times to get air, sat down in a chair to allow the breeze to hit my face. Ahh, fresh air. The vibrant breeze dried the sweat from my face and my dry mouth yearned for a sip of cool water as I closed my eyes. Low overcast clouds were forming overhead and I could see the traffic at the intersection of Grady and Fisher Streets. Crash! Bang! Screaming from the intersection. Directly in front of me were four people on the side of the road all on their cell phones. Two Hispanic women, one woman in an Indian headdress, and one man in jeans and a t-shirt. On the island in the middle of the street was an SUV that had hit a pedestrian. A sign pole had been knocked over, bent with flinging, exposed wires swinging in the wind. The pedestrian had been flung all the way over to the side of the road, but his shoe was still in the pedestrian strip. He lay flat with outstretched arms and blood rushing out from his head and arm.

When I saw that he looked Middle Eastern, I stopped my call. With what I had been through with Saudis and Middle Eastern students, I didn't feel any compassion. And why should I? He looked dead anyway. Ambulances and police cars rushed to the victim where a nurse from a nearby doctor's office had been doing chest compressions on the victim. The last bloody scene I had viewed was Loretta's bloody and gruesome murder photos – but those were just photos. This was playing out in front of me. As police officers attempted to speak with the bystanders, the EMS workers put a brace on his head and several others put his lifeless body on a stretcher. One young, female EMS worker kept holding his wrist checking his pulse. I felt no compassion for this individual as I thought, he probably caused the accident or was drunk or on drugs. Another squad car showed up, and a young officer along with a more seasoned one held out their arms to sterr onlookers back while they took the yellow tape, yanked the beginning of it, and started marking off the area. Confusion. Panic as people stopped to look and a TV station was setting up its equipment with a broadcaster interviewing several people. The commotion had also brought out people from the older run-down homes who stood on their porches, expressionless. An older lady in an apron motioned for her two young children, around 5 and 7, to go back into their home.

Mesmerized by the horrific scene, I told the students to continue working in their notebooks and dismissed them for their next class when the bell rang. It was my mid-day break, and I felt unaffected by it all. Empathy was foreign to me and I didn't care one bit.

After getting home and taking a nap, I wondered if Mike would be over with more videos this evening. Around dusk, my phone rang. "Maddie,"

"Yeah. I have some laryngitis, I'm sick."

"You sound bad."

"Yeah, I have some bug. Feel like I've been run over by a truck ... twice."

"Well, then you won't be too upset that we didn't do any questioning today."

"No, with the way I feel, I'm not upset, but what's the reason?"

"The agents had an urgent call about a drug bust down in Florence so that took priority."

"Oh, I see. When will the questioning begin again – tomorrow?"

"No, I doubt it. They're sorting through all of the paraphernalia and people they've takin' in.'"

"Well, I guess that's that."

Mike said apologetically, "I'll be checking in with you anytime I have something to tell you. You don't have to worry about that And take care of that cold. If you don't get better in a few days, I'd see a doctor."

"Thanks." And hanging up, I felt too ill to ponder the case and suspects because I only wanted to feel better.

CHAPTER TWENTY-NINE

Ian and I made a date to spend a day together and get to know each other better. I was thrilled to spend some time with him and tried *not* to get my hopes up that this would turn into a relationship. All I knew was that he was intriguing to me, and he had a sharp mind for analyzing cases. We planned to meet at the end of the lake and take a boat ride to sightsee into some inner places where people fished and camped out. I wondered if this trip was related to the investigation of any of the drug dealing that might be going on around the lake in the hidden coves where bikers and campers met in secret. An irrational thought – but a possibility. I took a bus down to the water's edge walked down the circular, concrete steps to the side of the lake. I was wearing shorts and a sleeveless top, and I felt the blazing sun on my shoulders and arms. Several women and families were on the sidewalk picking off pieces of bread from a little loaf and throwing it to the group of ducks bobbing up from the water. The ducks were quacking and darting for the bread while canoers were rowing in the distant current. I sat down on the last step in the shade and waited for Ian and the boat to dock. After about 10 minutes, the engine of the boat started getting louder and Ian touched me on my back and startled me.

"Ready for a boat ride today?" he chirped.

"I'm ready. It's a beautiful day to be on the water."

The boat scraped the side of the dock and then inched its way up to the side as the captain tied and secured the boat, and the riders walked from the boat onto the short plank and onto the sidewalk. Ian grabbed my hand, and we got in line to get on. The captain was dressed in long shorts and a t-shirt that covered his belly like a cloth over a bowl of fruit. Captain Jack had mousy gray whiskers and hair that squeezed out from underneath a tight cap that he would take on and off to wipe away the sweat from his forehead. Ian gave the captain two tickets and said to me, "I bought them from the merchant up at the vendor station," and I said, "Good thinking."

We walked down the aisle and took a seat under the canopy at the front of the boat. The rows of metal benches were filling up with passengers, and we moved inward to avoid the sun, but I said, "Getting wet on this day will feel good." Ian put his arm around me, and I watched as about twenty passengers got on board and took seats behind us. The captain untied the thick rope from the dock, and we listened as the loud engine started up. The boat moved forward and then we circled around to go back into the deepest part of the lake. The boat roared through the middle of lake and under the bridge and up into a remote area. We saw low-flying crows, turtles on rocks, and an occasional raccoon running along the banks. Several people were grilling outside their tent and campers were relaxing in lawn chairs, enjoying the day. Ian noted the shirtless men who were standing like statues, with hands on their hips, gazing at us as we passed. Even the wives and children of the men looked like wax mannequins as they prepared their meals on the grill and smoke billowed up, blowing a scent of meat our way.

Ian whispered to me, "Those guys look like they should be checked out. I have a weird feelin' about them."

I said, "Ian, let it go. And just enjoy the ride." He wasn't able to turn off his impression of people, even when he was off duty. We stayed on the boat another half hour or so and the splashes from the water on us felt like a water ride. We made it back to shore. The captain helped us off the boat and we walked down the dock area and back up to the kid's play area with water slides, where vendors frantically serviced all of the kids who were buying ice cream and snow cones.

Ian suggested, "Hey, since we're this far down the lake, I wanna show you a place that I own that is not too far from here."

Surprised, I said, "You own a home near here? I didn't know. . ."

"Yeah, it's not really a home built to rent out 'cause it's built for *security.*"

"Oh, for security? I'm curious. Show me this fortress." And I laughed not knowing what to expect.

****

On the way to White Oak in Ian's Lexus, we talked about the nice day and he told me about a home that he had been working on if there were ever an emergency. Who renovates a home just to have in case a catastrophe happens? Since most people didn't purchase a home to have as a spare baffled me. You've got to be convinced that the unthinkable will definitely happen.

Ian said, "I've been renovating this home for about five years now. It was a fixer upper, but it's almost done now."

"Five years to renovate a house? What took so long?"

"Well, it's *not* your ordinary house. It's been enhanced with extra security.

You'll see," And he smiled proud as a peacock over his accomplishment. I was really eager to see this man's castle. We rode through some winding roads back into a remote part of White Oak. We passed by several farms with chickens, and the stench of chicken poop caused me to roll up the window.

"Can you turn on the AC? That smells bad."

Ian said, "Don't worry. I don't have animals running wild on my land."

On the top of a curve was a hidden drive between two large oak trees, and we went far down the drive where a 1950s brick, ranch-style house lay in the middle of a cleared-off stretch surrounded by forest. The house was medium-sized, and despite the older facade, it had a garage adjacent to the house. He stopped at the end of the asphalt, and we walked onto a rickety deck up to the back door. He was thumbing through his keys to find the right key for the door.

Looking down at my foot that almost got caught between two deck boards, I said, "I thought that the renovations were almost complete."

Ian said, "Uh, that's just a cosmetic fix. The important renovations are almost done."

"And what are the important renovations?"

Just then, he opened the door, and we went in to a kitchen that had only a small table and two chairs. There were no appliances on the counter, and the linoleum was a dismal yellow with tan squares, reminiscent of the 1950s.

We went into the living room, and it was filled with supplies of every kind. It was a warehouse of ammunition, water jugs and canisters in stands, and plastic containers. It looked like a gun shop – a fancy gun shop – or a well-stocked hideout.

My mouth dropped open. "Wow, Ian, this place is a regular fallout shelter. You could survive here for weeks, or months." My head was canvassing the room that was stuffed with every kind of emergency supply – first aid kits, flashlights, batteries, stacks of sterno cups – there was no end to this stockpile.

Noticing the large plastic containers, I asked, "What's in those – more ammo?"

"No, it's freeze dried food. The kind that lasts for years and years – in case there's a dire emergency, it'll be there as a source of food."

"Just what kind of emergency are you anticipating if I may ask?" I was awestruck by this stockpile that was quite remarkable.

Ian said, "It's not just in my job but when I read the news about all of the possible, well, imminent, threats to this country, I can't sit by and not be prepared. It's only a matter of time before we're hit with a catastrophic event – and it will happen before this decade is out. I can guarantee you that."

With seriousness, I said, "You mean a terrorist attack . . ."

Ian bristled like an animal avoiding a predator. "I'm not saying that it will definitely be a terror attack. It could be any kind of attack. And attacking our banking system could wreak havoc and panic on all Americans. After a couple of days, people will want supplies, and those hungry people could turn into dangerous people. Anyone could inflict harm on someone else – if they're desperate enough."

I sat down on a fold-out chair next to a card table that had a two-way radio and some hand-held walkie talkies. I was absorbing everything he was telling me. After walking through the rooms of the house with shelves of stocked canned foods, he opened the door that led to the basement. He walked down the steps that were held on by a chain. The chain pinched my fingers as I grabbed it, and I slipped on each narrow step.

"Whew, it's chilly down here. It smells like chemicals, too."

Ian said, "A week ago, I had the workers line the inside with about a two foot wall of concrete to reinforce it. It could withstand a lot now. This is really the safest place since I haven't yet gotten the upstairs windows lined with plyboard."

I said, "This is amazing. You've got your bases covered if, God forbid, there's an emergency."

"Well, not really. I'd like to put a tall fence, the kind with spiked, metal bars at the top, around the entire lot and build up on some more ways to fend off attackers." Turning to me, he said, "Let me show you what I have outside."

We went back up the steps as I ended up onto the first floor. Ian grabbed my hand and led me outside to a hill that we climbed on a path through thick green grass. A black metal handle protruded up from the ground, and Ian said, "This is here if we need clean, potable water."

I noticed that he said "*we*" and then said, "Could people be in jeopardy of losing their drinking water?"

Ian said, "Anything could be targeted – water, food, and even banking systems could fail. And imagine the panic that would erupt after a few days when people can't get their money out. Pure chaos."

I took some of the water and splashed it on my face and said, "Ahhh, cool water. Nice."

We continued farther on up the hill to a level space where some archery targets had been set up on a flattened and dirt quadrant atop the hill. He had a small shed which he unlocked revealing bows and extra supplies.

There was every types of defense – bows and arrows, hatchets, slingshots – you name and he had it.

When he unlocked the door and I could see all of his weaponry, I laughed and said, "You could open up a summer camp for people prepping for anything." I picked up a bow, examined it, and said, "Can I try it out?"

"Sure. Only point that down at the target."

He showed me how to handle the bow and I tried to imitate him. "Is this it?" and Ian said, "Not exactly. Here, I'll show you." He then shot at the target and hit it straight on. I said, "That was terrific. OK, I'll try it." I took a minute to get set up. Swishhhhh! Ka-plunk! The arrow landed on the ground missing the target completely.

Ian said, "You've gotta take your time and aim – see the bull's eye."

"I thought that I did set up. Gimme another bow." I set up and ka-pluck!! The bow hit the target almost in the bull's eye but not quite.

Ian said, "That was better. It takes practice and patience."

"Yeah, I suppose if this is your weapon of choice."

We then headed to the trees in a dense patch along a path that went into the shaded part of the woods. Under these tall trees, there was no sunlight and day time could be confused with night time. Walking cautiously, I said, "This looks like a good place to get poison ivy. If I start itching . . ."

"Watch out for the plants with three leaves."

"They're all three leaves."

"Oh, stop complaining. See out here there's an abundance of ways to get food –nuts, berries, and animals."

"What kind of animals?"

Ian said, "Rabbits and insects and . . ."

"Eat rabbits? I couldn't. . ." I exclaimed.

"Well, if you want to survive, it might be necessary – that is, if you get really, really hungry."

Exasperated, I said, "I'll wait until that happens. If that day comes, I'll promise you that I'll learn to cook up this road kill dinner."

Ian said, "That might not be that far off."

I was starting to feel scared in this deserted area, and I said, "I'm ready to get back. I think I've had enough prepping education for one day." And I got on the path making a bee line for the exit outta there.

Disappointed, Ian said, "Aw, I didn't mean to frighten you. I was honestly trying to help you." He snagged my arm and pulled me toward him. We kissed for a long time leaning against a tree, I could feel his muscular body pushing toward me. After our exchange in the forest that day, we promised each other that we would never allow anyone to know about the two of us – at least while this case was ongoing. And I had sweet dreams of him that night.

CHAPTER THIRTY

May is a month of planning – planning vacations, summer work, internships, and even summer workshops to hone skills. Every May, I visited the local greenhouses and flower shops to find flowers to plant around my home and in the neighborhood. Gardening was a hobby to get me outside and although I didn't relish getting down in the dirt, when the flowers bloomed afterwards, it seemed worth the effort.

Days turned into weeks and with June around the corner, I was preoccupied with summer plans of what to do. I had almost forgotten about Mike and the murder investigation. School work and teaching was now heating up as teachers required more aides to help out with testing, and I was there to do what I could.

More international students were coming in which gave me some more hours at work to process them and get them into a mainstream classroom or to be with me in a more personal setting. I had the feeling that the students, even the capable ones, would rather be in a smaller setting than be treated like a deaf mute in the classroom because they couldn't always participate due to their lack of English skills. Another week came and went and school was out. Now, I had more free time to enjoy myself. I relaxed in solitude with a glass of wine and read spiritual books and listened to tapes. I heard a pastor on the radio who talked about a sense of peacefulness and acceptance of who you are, no matter what your status, gender, or whatever. Stretching out on the lawn chair with a glass of Merlot, I listened intently to the intriguing message. It was all about love, joy, and kindness to all.

Compassion and love for all mankind. He talked about how anyone that he knew who radiated love and compassion would not feel enmity from anyone or anything. His words added life and energy to my vapid life, and I was hooked on his materials. I felt totally relaxed in listening to suggestions for connecting with our spiritual side. Gazing up at the sky, the Carolina blue sky with puffy clouds spread to the faraway mountains, and I put another pillow behind my head for another hour of rest. Ring, ring, ring.

At first reluctant to answer, I said, "Yeah?" "Maddie, is that you?" said my friend Angie.

Angie was a friend that I had met through church events, and she gave me Biblical materials to read. She worked in sales, but her Biblical knowledge was phenomenal.

"Yep, it's me." "Where are you?" "I'm outside. . . getting a little R&R."

"Oh, well, I was wondering if you'd be up for going to church tomorrow?"

"Tomorrow? Yeah, I think that I can make it."

She laughed. "What else have got goin' on?" "That's true. What time should I meet you there?" "How about a little past 10 for the 10:15 service?"

"That's fine. See you there." After hanging up, I almost regretted having agreed, but was in a good mood with the weather and all.

****

I tossed and turned that night from the humidity and noise in the neighborhood. Boys across the street gunning their cars with no mufflers caused me to lie awake. I thought about taking a trip this summer and what I could do to fill my days. Getting up at midnight, I scanned the computer for places to visit and cruises. The price still was high, and I decided to wait a few weeks or month to see if the prices went down. At 8 the next morning, I went into my closet to find a summer dress to wear to church. I found a peach paisley dress and sandals and I ate a bowl of cereal before dashing off. Driving down Farrell Street, the nice shops and clothing stores deteriorated every mile into smaller shops inches from the street. Stores with broken windows, faded signs, and people loitering out front gave me an uneasy feeling. Graffiti marked at least every other building, as the street got narrower and narrower. I checked to make sure my door was locked and inched closer and closer, moving in anticipation of the traffic light turning green. Three cars in front of me were turning into the parking lot and I followed. The church was on the side and since it wasn't quite time for church – the lot was vacant. I went to the side door to meet Angie. A Gothic-style, charcoal-colored church with its grand pillars and ornate architecture of flying buttresses and gargoyles. Triangular, slender, opaque windows adorned each side of the church and purplish-blue hydrangea lined the sides. Grassy areas in between the parking lot and church were moist as trees shaded it and kept it barren of grass. Only a small cemetery is behind the church and the few gravestones, inscribed with only names and dates, were worn down from outside elements. A person would have to get very close to read them.

Waiting for Angie at the door, I heard a "Hey, I'm in here. Whaddya doin' outside?"

Angie had been waiting inside, and she held the door as we walked through the vestibule to the spacious foyer.

A high ceiling kept the room cool and the sun shone through the rectangular panes of glass onto a mosaic floor below. Hanging chandeliers were mere ornaments since there was plenty of light from above. Magnolias in crystal vases placed in inlays around the church permeated the air with sweet smells. After saying hello to several churchgoers and ushers, we took our bulletins and made our way to the pews off to the side. Compared to the foyer, the sanctuary was tenebrous and somber. I had to shift my position to get comfortable on the hard wood pew, due to the curved back. I was on the end adjacent to stained glass windows and dusty molding.

Angie said, "I think that Pastor Freeman is here today."

As the organ bellowed out, we all stood and sang a hymn.

At the end of the hymn, Pastor Freeman in his white robe took to the podium and belted out, "This is the day the Lord has made. Let us be glad in it."

We greeted each other, repeated verses, and listened to the sermon. Pastor Freeman began with his sermon. My mind was wandering as he began to speak.

Why had I even come here today? There didn't seem to be any point to it. He talked about his garden at home and how he and his wife were having problems with the seeds sprouting, but he said there was no need to fret. He also talked about how he had to have a landscaper put up a good fence and gate to keep out animals. It wasn't until he started saying with conviction, "*Enter through the narrow gate. For wide is the gate and broad is the road that leads to destruction, and many enter through it. But small is the gate and narrow the road that leads to life, and only a few find it.*"

Chills went up my spine and little goose bumps tingled down my arms and legs. What this a coincidence? I don't know, but it was eerie. I sat up and listened more intently. Pastor Freeman discussed how it is not what we accomplish or all of our good works that get us through that narrow gate. Instead, we get through that narrow gate with unconditional love, compassion, and forgiveness. And most of all, faith. With his occasional quick look at the congregation, it felt like he was speaking directly to me – in all ways. I felt changed by his words, and I desired to hear more but in a matter of minutes, the sermon was over. As we sang, Angie smiled at me, and we left to meet at a Thai restaurant. We got in our cars and taking I-75 South met downtown.

Angie and I always liked Samyan Restaurant and Thai food. Round tables under small trees made the atmosphere conducive to quiet chats. A Thai waitress showed us to a table outside near the water and we made ourselves comfortable in the bamboo chairs. The waitress gave us some shrimp rolls with soy sauce and brought us tangy, peach-colored Thai iced tea that I drank quickly.

Angie said, "Did you enjoy church today?"

"Yeah, it was enlightening."

"You seem interested."

"I've been thinking about that same verse lately about the narrow gate that he preached on, and what he was saying hit me."

Changing the subject, Angie said, "Yeah, that was interesting. He speaks in figuratives. So what have you got on your calendar for later this week and summer?"

"Uh, I dunno, probably the same ol' vacation to the beach and . . ."

"You should get more involved with charities. They are terrific for meeting new people." Unexcited, I said, "What kinds of charities?"

"Well, there's the American Cancer Society, the Red Cross, and the American Heart Association, and ALS, ya know, the charity for Lou Gehrig's patients."

Hesitant, I said, "I dunno."

Angie said, "You should think about it. Sometime this week, I'm gonna get out my book and give you the name of someone that would love for you to volunteer."

At the word "volunteer," I wanted to back out, but Angie was being too nice for me to snub her charities.

Deferring, I said, "If they really do need the help, then I'd like to volunteer."

I was surprised at my own willingness to get involved but was talked into it. And what did I have to lose? If it helped me to meet people, then maybe it would be worth it. Angie and I ate the cashew chicken and succulent noodles, and I had some renewed optimism for the week.

CHAPTER THIRTY-ONE

Monday morning sprang into motion, and I called Mike for an update on the case. I sensed that I would be hearing from him and that there would be some break in the case. I thought it must be him when I heard my phone ring, but it was only private tutoring agencies wanting a summer tutor. I took a walk down the path leading to the forest across the adjacent field. Several deer pranced onto the road and stopped. A large deer followed by three skeletal doe dashed to the other side of the road and through the bushes out of sight. They were beautiful creatures and I adored their gracefulness. I walked down the path to the gazebo and settled myself on the bench inside. The heat of the sun was burning my neck and ears. After resting and watching the birds landing on the edges, I laid back against the railing to see a pit bull angling toward me, swaggering back and forth in order to scope me out. Afraid to take any action to make the dog lunge at me, I slowly pastor had said about when you love all creatures, people will fail to show enmity in return, then this would be the time for me to use that principle of thought energy. I reached out to the dog and believing that this must be someone's beloved pet, I put my hand near its nose. The dog merely sniffed my hand and ran down the path, and it was gone. Poof! Like that, a potential for real harm had ceased to be any threat to me. But my quixotic attempt to get out of a situation was using my thoughts, and to some that might seem incredulous. Nevertheless, I was out of danger. I reached into my pocket to get my cell phone to make a report a stray dog to the SPCA, Where's my phone? I rubbed against every side of both pockets and it wasn't there. I briskly jogged home to look for my phone. Running up the steps, I found it on the ottoman with a message that I had a call – Mike's number.

Pressing call back, he said with an unusual energy, "Maddie I have news about the case. It may be big . . ."
"What is it?"

"It appears that there was some connection between some student and Loretta Bryson. There is some evidence of grades being changed –compromising the GPAs and . . ."

"I knew it. A money scheme to get passing grades."

"It doesn't necessarily mean that any students were involved in her murder, but it does shed some light on shady practices in that department."

"How did the agents get this info?" "There were some students who were obviously jealous that they weren't getting the grades so they went to Administration."

"Who were they?"

"We don't know for sure. It's all unfolding."

"Admin knew about it and didn't say or do anything?"

"They were in the middle of doing their own investigation when the murder occurred and . . . And here's the kicker. There's some talk about who might have started that fire and they're talking to a student who may give us some information."

"And it was all covered up so they wouldn't have to admit to an arson and cheating." I gasped.

"Maddie, keep this quiet for now and let it play itself out. Both agents will get to the bottom of the fire and who was involved and what the deal was exactly."

"How are they goin' to do that?" "Believe me, they have been trained in making people talk."

"Can we go and take a look at the crime scene again? I have this feelin' that we should give it a once-over just to be sure."

"Sure of what? It's been scoured into every corner by officers, agents, and forensics."

"I dunno. I'm relying on my female intuition." "What is that intuition tellin' you?"

"It's sayin' that it couldn't hurt to see it with different eyes."

"Those people in forensics are the best. They look at every hair, every fiber, . . ."

"Pleeease. It wouldn't hurt to take a look at it. I wanna go with you and see it for myself."

"I'll have to ask the agents to let us in because it's still quartered off with crime scene tape. But they are re-opening the building soon to the public, in the next day or two. Geez, I hate to ask. They'll think we're mighty presumptuous."

"Since you're doing the questioning there anyway, it wouldn't take but five minutes."

Placating me, Mike said, "OK. I'll set something up. Let you know."

Upbeat, I said, "Now we're getting' somewhere. Bye."

Unenthusiastic, Mike said, "Will let you know when I know."

****

Checking my emails, I got endless junk mail. Angie sent me an email with an inspirational picture and verse. She wrote me that she was thinking about me and suggested that I get out and contribute to something that would lift my spirits. I almost resented the suggestion of doing something for nothing. Doing more volunteer work didn't interest me. It was too much of a hassle and let it go. I'd get to it another day. Off to the Winton Woods to take another jog. Breaking through puffy, celestial clouds, the sun made a timid debut on sparkling waters and the bridge that glistened in the distance. As I started down to the fishing area, I held onto the handrail as winds picked up and blew my hair straight back. Sailboats were tossing and bouncing on the waves and fishermen were holding onto the sails with all their might. I made a semi-circle around this side of the lake and up the hill around to the stage where local musicians had their Friday night concerts. Coming around the bend, I took a seat on the end of the stage and watched as the pontoon boat captain docked his boat and riders anxiously exited the plank onto the walkway on the river's edge. They looked relieved to be off the boat as some of them held onto their caps and hats in the wind. Overhead, the once cerulean blue had turned dark blue and ominous. Zipping my windbreaker and feeling the occasional drip of rain, I pulled the hood over my head. Clap, rumble -- a storm was upon me. I ran to my car and got home in no time flat. In a matter of minutes, I was in the thick of a major storm and flung open my front door which swung so hard that it hit the wall. I leaned on it, pushed it shut, and locked it. The blinds in the hallway windows were flapping and I secured them tightly to hold them down and getting damaged.

The weather radio on the baker's rack had gotten so dirty that I brushed it off and turned it on. Loud static and a recorded message said, "Winds are recorded at 60 miles per hour and are picking up around the Indiana border. Seek shelter in a building as winds and hail could cause damage to persons and animals. Do seek shelter in low-lying areas. . ." I gathered up my cell phone, weather radio, and pillow and blanket and locked myself in my storage room for a turbulent night of incessant lightning, crackling tree branches and windows that had cracked from the tornado that ripped through with unprecedented force. In the morning, the neighborhood was deathly quiet as leaves and branches covered the roads, driveways, and flower garden. A window with cracked lines looked like striated streaks from broken capillaries in an injured eyeball. Trash cans and flower pots were in unfamiliar places and several neighbors farther down the street were straightening up their yard and picking up debris. It was like emerging to a new world that I had survived. Throughout the night I heard police sirens and ambulances and I hunkered down in solitude. In the kitchen, digital clocks on appliances blinked from the power loss that had been restored in the wee hours of the morning. After re-setting the clocks, I turned on the TV to newscasts on every station showing mobile homes that were nothing but heaps of rubble and kids who were crying. I was moved by the demolished areas and all of the people who had been affected. My home was still intact as was everything inside. I was disturbed by the sights and I wanted to help. Perhaps I could take Angie's advice and do some volunteer work to help out people who were less fortunate. I decided to give the charities a call tomorrow to see what I could do.

Skimming my emails, I found the numbers of the charity coordinators and jotted the phone numbers down. I wasn't able to reach any of the homeless or pantry charities by phone, so I tried the ALS charity next. I almost hung up when a sweet voice picked up.

The secretary answered. "ALS Cincinnati. How may I help you?"

"Yes, this is Maddie Hauck, and I was given this number by my friend Angie Smythe. She told me to get in touch with the head coordinator for volunteer programs if I wanted to volunteer."

"Oh so you'd like to help us – with fundraising, our ALS Walk, or with public relations?"

"Oh, I dunno. When is the Walkathon?"

"It's in October on a Saturday."

"Could I possibly attend one of your meetings to get a feel for what I'd like best and what I could contribute . . . ?"

"That's so nice of you. We could always use an extra set of helping hands."

"When is your next meeting?"

"Let me check our calendar here. We have meetings in September, February, and May."

"So I guess I should attend the upcoming meeting in September." "That would be correct. Then you could see what is involved in the Walkathon. Could I have your email and phone number? That way I can contact you for when and where that takes place."

"Certainly."

I gave her my email and phone.

She said, "God bless you honey," and I spent most of the rest of the day in a better mood.

CHAPTER THIRTY-TWO

That night I watched a movie by myself and dropped off to sleep. I envisioned how the fall would soon be coming and I'd have some fulfilling volunteer work in the fall. I awoke instantly and looking around the room I felt that an entire night had passed, but it was only 2:30. Although I wasn't sick I felt nauseous with a rumbling stomach that made me want some carbonated beverage to sip to alleviate the nausea. I just didn't feel right and too many conflicting thoughts were plaguing me and upsetting my rest. Suddenly it popped into my head! The ALS charity met only in September, February, and May. How could Adrianna be at an ALS meeting in December? That's where she claimed to be the night of the murder. She could possibly be meeting in preparation for some other event but I kept reflecting on every word that I could remember her saying, how she said it, and her posture. She emanated confidence and honesty. The night hours ticked by. Three o'clock, four o'clock, five o'clock. . . I knew that I had to make some calls – to whom? The charity, Mike, I didn't know. After telling myself that this was probably nothing, I dozed off again to awaken around 8 am and I staggered into the shower to wake myself up. I reviewed the ALS website again and all of the information that I could get from it. Just didn't seem right. I was troubled and confounded by Adrianna's story. She was controlled and self-assured during the interview and ruled out, but how could they really rule out anyone? And who would suspect her? But how could she pull something like that off all on her own? I recalled that she had a boyfriend who was a bodybuilder. I think his name was Bradley.

I kept shaking my head in disbelief. This didn't seem possible nor plausible but it just didn't add up. What was behind it? At 10 on the dot, I made the call to the ALS Foundation.

A lady with a slow drawl answered. "ALS Foundation of Cincinnati. This is Betty."

"Yes, this is Maddie Hauck and I talked to someone yesterday about doing some volunteer work for ALS and I wanted to know. Do you have meetings in December?"

"In December. No, ma'am, not December. That's a holiday month with so much going on that our members are so busy it would be difficult to get together, so we don't typically have anything then."

"Oh, I was curious, that's all. Thanks."

"No problem sweetie." And I was in shock. I wanted to get in touch with Mike but he wasn't picking up and his office phone had the answering machine. I called twice before leaving a message. On another case – a bigger case no doubt. Nervous about what to do with this, I fidgeted until I got a text from him.

The text read, "Will re-open bldg later this week. Investigation of crime scene OK with agents. Meet me there tomorrow at 8 am."

With pouring rain the next morning, I pulled on my rain boots and long rain jacket and wrapped and tied it with a knot. For a second, I reminded myself of the detective on the lunch box that I had when I was a child. With umbrella in hand, I made my way out to the car and downtown. I was waiting for 10 minutes before Mike showed up at 8:10. Standing hunched under the ledge above, I stood back from the students who crowded the sidewalks with their overstuffed backpacks.

I was so anxious to talk that babbling came out of my mouth. "I *have to* talk to you about Adrianna. I think that there's something about her story that *doesn't* add up."

To my surprise, Mike said, Shhhhh. Not now. Here come the agents to let us in. Talk later, in *private.*"

I was dumbfounded and shut my mouth because his tone of voice made me think that I was somehow compromising the case. The agents walked up to the two front double doors.

Agent Garrett said, "Let's make this quick so we can get to the task at hand today." I couldn't tell if their silence was their perfunctory style or they were ticked off at our request. The agents pushed aside the crime scene tape, and we followed them down the hall. Mike was directly behind them and my galoshes squeaked loudly as I trailed behind, controlling my steps not to fall on the wet, slick tiles. The lights inside were bright, in comparison to outside, where dark skies made 8 am seem as dark as 10 pm. Opening the door, Mike went to the computer, took off the plastic cover, turned it on, and started looking through the desk drawers. Agents Garret and Ian looked at each other in discontent. They turned and went down the hall and I didn't care. While Mike went through some papers in the desk, I sifted through papers on top of the file cabinets. The florescent light flickered and a bulb went out which made me jump but Mike was on a hunt – oblivious to it. After about twenty minutes, we switched places and he was making a circle around the room bending over and around to look behind the chairs and file cabinets. We weren't uncovering anything that could shed light on the case. Nada, nothing. Another half hour went by with our searching in silence with total concentration of turning up anything. Mike's phone rang.

The phone's volume was turned up so high that I was able to hear Agent Nelson's voice. "Y'all just about finished up there?"

Mike said, "Well, we have a few more areas to check and then we're done."

"That's it? We don't get any more time?"

"We can't stay here all day. Besides, they've been through here with a fine tooth comb, so is there for us to do?" Despite the clammy, cold air, I was sweating and overheated with drops of sweat trickling onto my coat. This was our last chance to turn up anything.

After a few minutes, Mike said impatiently, "I've gotta get goin'. There's nothin' here that I can find."

He started putting the plastic back over the computer, resolute that it was the end of our search. He said, "C'mon, let's go," and I got up and went to the door as he locked it from the inside and started to pull the the door shut. I was hesitant to leave and unwilling to throw in the towel. I moved slowly and reluctantly to the door. Peering through the glass panes in the door, I saw something on the floor next to the wheel on the bottom of the desk.

I pleaded, "Wait, wait, there's something under the desk that's shining."

"Probably a paper clip . . . or staple."

Begging, I said, "I just want to see what it is." Getting down and pinching the little object that was stuck in the wheel, I could see that it was a little plastic ball... with blood on it.

Mike asked, "What is that? A button?"

"No, it looks like it came off a bracelet or . . . and it has blood on it.

"How could they miss that? If there's blood on it, then it's part of the evidence that . . ."

Holding it close to my eye, I said, "It's from some kind of jewelry."

Mike was astonished and confused. He turned the lights back on and was anxious to search again.

Incredulous, he said, "This has never happened to me in all of the years that I've been investigating."

We were both on our knees, with eyes an inch from every corner of the desk, hunting for more evidence. He handed me a handkerchief and said, "Don't touch any more evidence. Use this." While Mike was turning the wheels around and picking what looked like pieces of hairs strands, I was in the chair behind the desk opening each drawer.

Slowly pulling out the top drawer, I squealed, "Look, another bead!! And it has some blood on it!" Pulling out a handkerchief and picking up the bead, I placed it in Mike's palm which was also covered with a handkerchief. The next ten minutes we went over the desk and the area around it but didn't find another thing.

Mike called Agent Garrett and said, "I need you to get down here. We found something that you should see."

Agent Garrett said, "What is it?" Mike said, "It's definitely evidence. They're two petite beads with blood."

Perplexed, Ian said, "Where did you find them?"

Fired up, I said, "*We* found them down in the desk's wheel and in the small crevice in the desk drawer."

Agent Garrett said, "We'll transport this to the forensics lab and get this into processing. This opens the case wide. Blood and everything."

Weak and trembling, I sat down in a student desk in the hallway and watched as Mike and the agents talked inside the office. Their conversation was only background murmuring. I put my head down, took deep breaths, and processed everything. The ALS meeting and Adrianna's lie, the beads . . . Oh my God, Adrianna was involved in the murder. I was stunned and unable to move. Clutching the raincoat tie around my waist and swallowing to get the words out of my mouth, I went to the office.

With my hand over my mouth and shaking, I said, "It was Adrianna. The beads are from what she was wearing the night of the murder. And she lied about where she was the night of the murder."

Ian said, "What are you trying to tell me?"

"I'm saying that Adrianna was not at any ALS meeting and those beads are from her hair barrettes." The agents and Mike gasped in shock.

Agent Garrett said, "If she's right, then we've gotta get to Adrianna and check this out.... now. Follow us."

CHAPTER THIRTY-THREE

The agents stormed out and Mike and I ran to our cars parked on the side of the street. The agents did a u-turn in the middle of the street and Mike was right on them as we sped down the street getting through the lights as they turned red just to keep up. Down Newbury Street onto Bledsoe Avenue. 218 Bledsoe Avenue. That was the number in my dream, 2-1-8. Too much of a coincidence. We went up and down some small hills as I felt my stomach rise and fall with every bounce and jump from the hilly streets. Agent Garrett slammed on the brakes and parked zigzag in front of an old, colonial style house. The agents jumped out and adjusted their coats as if positioning weapons inside their holsters. Ian called for backup, while Agent Garrett was banging on the door for an answer. Bradley, Adrianna's boyfriend, stuck his head out of an upstairs window and yelled down that he was coming down to open up the door.

Upon opening the door, the agents yelled, "Where's Adrianna Smythe? Who are you?"

"She's, she's on the back porch. I can get her."

But the agents were already running down the hallway with their shoes stomping on the wood floors. Pushing open an old door to an outside screened porch they looked out to find Adrianna in shorts and halter top sipping a drink sprawled out on a lounge chair. She jumped back dropping her magazines and papers.

She edged backward in fright and screamed, "Who are you? What are you doing . . ?"

From the front door, I could see Agent Garrett grabbing her by the arm and lifting her out of the chair and through the house to a side room.

Ian said to Bradley, "Let's go," and he told him to take a seat on the sofa in the living room.

Agent Garrett started the interrogation in a loud voice. "Where were you the night of Loretta Bryson's murder?"

Bradley, nervous leaned back against the seat cushions as to get away. "I was at the gym . . . the gym that I bought and manage."

Ian said, "Well, you've gotta prove that."

Terrified, Bradley said, "I can show you what I was doing that night. I was at the gym setting up rooms for red light therapy, installing some more massage chairs."

As I stood at the front door, I could see the inside of the living room and down the hall. The living room was sparsely decorated and had a futon, a hard back chair and several small pictures. There was a framed Teacher of the Year certificate that said "Adrianna Smythe" in the corner and a small shelf with some trophies from Bradley's days when he competed in wrestling tournaments.

Agent Garrett had stopped questioning Adrianna and was rummaging through drawers and through purses. Sliding open the closet doors, he searched every shelf until he held up a pair of sparkly high-heeled shoes. "Well, well, look what we have here – a pair of shoes with a point on the heel that has a little blood on it."

Adrianna burst into tears. Bradley trembled. And we stood stunned.

Ian took out a plastic bag and Agent Garrett dropped the shoes into the bag and zipped it shut. While Agent Nelson marked and labeled the bag, Agent Garrett proceeded to go through a jewelry box, and Mike stood with his arm in front of Bradley as to shield him from making any rash moves.

Agent Garrett pulled out some burettes from the jewelry box and said, "This must be our lucky day. We've hit the jackpot with evidence. Hhmm, burettes – and several beads are missing. Get another bag" He carefully dropped the burettes in another bag.

Agent Garrett then stepped into the hallway and took out a black duffel bag and unzipped it. Inside, there was a dumbbell with two small strands of hair and blood on the end. "It keeps comin'."

Mike said, "We've got back up on its way."

Agent Garrett said, "Ms. Smythe, it's time for you to tell us what happened that night."

Adrianna was flailing her arms in a panic. "I can't, I can't tell you . . ."

Ian contritely said, "You have to tell us. We already know."

Adrianna, brushing back her hair and wiping her eyes, said, "Bradley needed the money 'cause his gym wasn't doin' so good. So some Chinese students were desperate for grades so they paid us so they wouldn't get deported. Loretta found out and she was planning to turn us in."

Bradley, resembling a mad man biting his lip, was restrained by Mike.

Ian said, "Any Saudi students involved?'

Adrianna said, "No. It was a group of Chinese students. I swear they were the only ones who were paying us."

Mike said, "Who were they?"

In a hushed manner, Adrianna was speaking in a strange and monotone voice. "It was the group that hung out together on campus – Yuki, Dao-ming, Kym, Lian, Sunni, and the rest of 'em. Sunni's father funded it because he owned an electric company in China. He had deep pockets and gave us whatever we wanted."

Brad yelled, "No, no . . ." and lunged toward Agent Garrett from behind attacking him and punching him, digging his fingers into his eyes from behind. Before Ian could react, I pulled out my taser and shot Bradley directly in the middle of his back.

Ka-zooomm. A cloud of smoke lingered and then disintegrated into air from the taser's discharge. Bradley screamed and fell to the floor. He convulsed and jolted his arms and legs. His torso flapped like a fish. He groaned in sheer pain. Ian assisted Agent Nelson to a chair and Mike ran and got a towel from the kitchen and put it over Agent Garrett's eyes.

Agent Garrett with face buried in the towel muffled, "I think I'm OK."

The taser smoke left after the shot stretched from the gun to Bradley. I pointed the gun down and observed the scene. It was over. Police cars and ambulances surrounded the house, and the mob of officers and medics with gloved hands darted to Agent Garrett and Bradley. Officers handcuffed Adrianna and Bradley was led them away with the help of Ian and two other officers.

An officer said to me, "I'm gonna need to take that taser," and I handed it to him. The case was solved and I was free from it. Sweet freedom.

CHAPTER THIRTY-FOUR

After everyone had left, Mike and I went out into the front yard in awe. People had stopped on the sidewalk and neighbors were on their front steps, motionless and speechless. With hands over our brows shading our eyes from the sun, we were motionless as the commotion ended and peace was restored.

Mike said, "Thanks for helping. You were pretty fast with that taser."

I was oblivious to what he was saying. I muttered, "It was the Chinese students who were behind it. I can't believe it. I was so sure that the Saudi students were behind the whole thing." I held my head and dropped to my knees onto the cool, wet grass. The shock had overtaken me and I was immobilized.

Mike knelt down beside me and was stroking my back. He said, "It certainly pointed to the Saudi students, but *anyone* can get caught up in something that they desperately want. Believe me, anyone is capable of doing the most unethical, immoral acts.... even murder."

"Yeah, but I didn't understand how other students, the ones that claimed to be the ones that had everything going for 'em could get into such a horrible plan."

Mike said, "They were tempted and Adrianna and her boyfriend were just there and willing to take the money. Money motivates people to things they wouldn't otherwise do."

He helped me up with my unsteady knees wobbling to stand up.

I said, "Can you take me home? I've gotta get cleaned up."

Mike led me by the hand and he took me home without saying a word during the drive. He walked me to the door and opened it for me. Dazed, I said, "I'm gonna take a long bath and rest."

Mike said, "When you're up to it, we'll settle up all of this *officially*." He left and I went upstairs, threw myself on the bed and wept for hours. The magnitude of what had happened had all come out and I knew that the Chinese student who had "fallen" from the garage landing had most likely been a suicide. And I grieved for that person. What a waste for anyone to throw themselves to their death because of life's expectations thrust upon them. If he had only seen that he was good enough as he was, then there might not have been the deadly outcome. I'll never forget the poor souls caught up in this senseless tragedy.

CHAPTER THIRTY-FIVE

For days, I was unable to go out and resume my normal schedule. I hung around my home and didn't take care of myself. My hair, tousled and tangled with black circles under my eyes, made me look like a homeless person. I was depressed and back on the meds again although they didn't help. I felt stuck in some kind of hole of sadness that had swept me in. People didn't understand what this felt like until they are actually in it. On the verge of tears all the time, I felt like a burden to everyone around me. I was suicidal.

When the seasons started changed and friends started calling to check on me, I decided to go to church for some kind of healing. It seemed pointless, but I wanted to find some answers to questions about life's meaning and purpose. Most of all, I wanted to discover who I really was in this crazy world. I spent days medicating myself with narcotics that I had gotten from a doctor and taking a sleeping pill when I wanted to do harm to myself.

I didn't phone or text friends for days, they all showed up at my home one by one telling me that I needed to get help. Looking around at church support groups, I finally found a support group that helped people with the narcotics, depression, and anxiety. The last thing in this world I wanted to do was share my innermost thoughts with people whom I thought would never understand, so I would mark my calendar and then cross it off when I couldn't bear to attend. When I finally got the courage to go to a meeting, I sat in the parking lot staring at the clock until it was close to the time that the meeting would begin, and then I'd walk to the door with heavy heart and with plenty of hankies in case I cried. Everyone at the meeting sat in a semi-circle with the lead person at the front. The people were all so comforting supporting me and calling me by name with each subsequent visit. It was the third meeting, and taking my usual seat on the end of the semi-circle, Agent Garrett caught my eye as he entered and quickly looked for a place to sit. His expression was more of a fearful child than an agent. While introducing himself, he made the remark that anyone could wind up in a support group – it didn't matter who you were, your income, or social status. His facial expressions were more personal, and he would laugh when someone would make a joke about something. After the meeting, we spoke for a short time, and I was glad that I met him despite the circumstances.

Entering through the narrow gate and the meaning of it pondered on my mind, and I decided to talk to my pastor after church about the meaning of it. In describing the events of my life, I called Pastor Freeman about how I had devalued and been suspicious of people because of what had happened to me in the past. His helpful words were that our past experiences color and shape our lives today. It is through our pain and experiences that we interpret our lives and world. He said that we are welcome to enter through that narrow gate but we have to want to go through it. It was reassuring to me that the gate is open to *ALL* who desire that narrow path and not the wide path which is what most people only know.

He said, When God closes a door, he opens a wider gate."

I also decided to start back to church, and in entering the church, I saw a poor woman who was sweeping the steps of the church and realized that no matter your humble beginnings, *everyone* has the choice of which gate to enter.

Life is short, so make of it what you can and choose what gate you will enter.

And after church, I went home and later rested – truly rested – with my dog Sylva.

READER'S GUIDE

1. What are Maddie's problems physically, spiritually, and emotionally? How does she deal with her problems and change throughout the story?

2. What adjectives would you use to describe the main characters?

3. What figurative language did you notice throughout the story? How does figurative language add to the descriptions?

4. What is your impression of Granny Mildred? How does she help (or hurt) Maddie in her journey to make sense of the world?

5. What do you think *entering through the narrow gate means?* And what could we all learn from this proverb?

Printed in the United States
By Bookmasters